We're Going To Need The Girls

Martha Tembo

For Mum and Dad

My Constant Support and The Inspiration Behind My
Imagination

And Thank You Diana for helping me get here

Contents

Glossary

Shikulu - Grandfather

Chibuku – Traditional beer

Mwata – Head Chief

Mama – Grandmother

Chitenge - African fabric

Ubupe – Gift

Ba Mpundu – Twins

Shinganga – Medicine man

Ubutanda – Straw mat

Nkobekela - Fiancée

Na – Mother of

Shi – Father of

Foundations

Shikulu (grandfather) is the historical root that has dominated our most recent history, he did something unusual for our people, he created his own image, he painstakingly protected and repeated the story he wanted us to know of him and lived by that unwaveringly. But said very little about his life before his return from the Great War. Even less detail was shared surrounding his transition into his headmaster post. A position that would eventually make him central to the lives of everyone in the community. During that time, we did not share stories to be recalled in the way people of foreign culture stored and preserved stories of those that came before them.

Shikulu shared only the names of relatives he deemed necessary for the advancement of his vision, and facts given were dispassionate. He did this even as he shared the story of how his mother and father died, an event that led to him living among Christian missionaries. How he lived, the surroundings, what he felt, who was good, who was bad, kind or frightening, were not considered useful details he felt the need to pass on to the next generation. As a result, Shikulu is only known in part. His people only got a feel of the essence of his heart later in life, after he returned from the Great War, where he returned possessed, by the unabating pursuit to free our people from imperialism. His experience in the war had awakened clear understanding, not possessed in him prior to that experience that all of them were sleeping walking into permanent subjugation. He chose intellectual warfare as the most effective method to apply, over physical assault which he was sure would be necessary later. At the end of his service during the Great War, he lived in constant worry of the things he had learned about the people we had found ourselves entangled with. He had watched their methods and knew that if we failed to plan and act sooner rather than later, we would lose everything that we were.

He became driven and fixated on detail, however minor because he believed everything had to be precise if we were going to succeed. He also felt strongly that the timing of the moment to make our move, was crucial to ensure success. More than anything he was convinced that everything in his plan had to be in place before any moves for freedom could be made, he refused to accept any alternative measures to what he had in mind. In his plan it was essential that more people than be made ready to fight when the time was right. His emphasis on detailed preparation, was a mantra repeated over and over and heard by anyone who would listen. We learned later that whilst this was his passion, there was by no means communal agreement in the community with him, a fact that did not matter to him. Convinced that his plan was the best way forward and he stood firm in that belief, despite objections, questioning or doubt by others. Shikulu was not sensitive to the idea he might need to adapt his approach to suit others around him, or concerned with making his ideas more inclusive of the way his people thought and operated at that time. Planning for the whole was a communal act, the idea that they could be expected to follow one man with a vision that he refused to share in its entirety was not how things were done for several reasons.

His refusal to work within established structures to achieve his goal, would eventually result in numerous fractures between him and others in the village. The unrest over strategy and direction would later make its way into his home, with his own sons questioning his timelines and asking him to reconsider. His sons would eventually grow impatient and join the freedom fighting movement building within the country. Shikulu was naturally averse to seeking counsel, and his blind spot was his arrogance. In not trusting others with the details of his plans, preferring to lead and know everything alone, he unwittingly caused mistrust among his people who as a result, who questioned his sincerity in wanting what was best for everyone. In the end they developed a filter for his advice, choosing to execute only what they believed to be the best actions for the community and ignoring the rest of what he had to say despite his insistence that all his instructions had to be executed for everything to come together in an orderly fashion at the end.

Shikulu was not from the region he ultimately settled with his wife and children; he was from Congo. His children identified as such and would pass this identity on to their children. The truth was prior to the new arrivals, people moved freely, our history had always been one of movement, until they enforced borders. Movement remains imprinted in our DNA, even our souls. However, having no regard for other cultures, they did not know or care that they were condemning generations to a life of restlessness. To this day, the majority of us retain an internal longing for movement and exploration of new places. If we could, we would still travel and move to new regions every few years.

Shikulu was one of nine children. His father Kunda was part of the Chieftain, his mother Kalwe, like most women and young children, worked on the fields in which everyone in the community had a share in the produce. The village they lived on was called Mitondo. From what he remembered life flowed along in an unvaried and predictable routine, which was not dissimilar to life before them or before that. This familiarity and continuity within the community, provided a sense of security. The day's activities and responsibilities, where clear from dawn until it came time to retire and sleep. Everyone understood their roles, most were happy with the music note that represented their contribution to life in their community. Families tended to prioritise passing on skills and training to their immediate

11

members, knowledge involving contribution to the village was handed down from one generation to the next. It was not unusual for families to be known to specialise in one type of specific skill or trade. Land was never owned but respected and farming was done with the awareness of rotation which included leaving farmland to just be, for it to regenerate. Before any of the people of this period were even conceived, an understanding had been reached about who would occupy which compound within the village and what specialist skill they would bring as a family or as individuals to add to the whole.

Cooking was an outdoor activity on a charcoal stove, all cooking was done before sundown to take advantage of the natural light, another reason for this practice was to reduce the likelihood of attacks from unseen predators enticed by the aroma. Daytime cooking also minimised incidents of rodents becoming a problem within the community, as the clearing up could be better carried out while there was still light. Rules surrounding how the cooking was done to keep the community clean were established years before any of them were born, as was the case with most of the knowledge and understanding they had of the ways in which they lived. Important times and appropriate behaviours were repeated and reinforced through verbal instruction, this was done in form of stories and song for the memory of village safety to continue its flow seamlessly.

If you asked and no one ever did, but if you did, none of the people would have been able to recall an instance in their lifetime when they had witnessed an attack on one of them as a result of outdoor cooking. There had been the usual tragedies, falls, burns, sickness induced by ingesting the wrong root or fruit, bites from mini beasts were to be expected. Incidents of miscarriage was often ascribed to infidelity by the husband during pregnancy. Twins were a bad omen and upon birth both babies would be given a concoction to take, that would cause them to fall sleep permanently. This was not perceived as wrong and the fact that twins or more, were a rare occurrence confirmed the belief that they were not a good omen. Conditions such as mental illness were understood and supported by the time the people of the current community had been born. However, the village rule was to discourage reproducing with a person known to be mentally unwell or disabled to stop the continuation of the condition.

This was done to protect the general health and spirituality of the community. All men were required to be truthful in the event they impregnated women who were not their wives, especially when the relationship was unknown to the people. This was to avoid the remote chance of siblings unknowingly engaging in sexual activity with each other, procreation or intercourse of this kind was forbidden. It was widely accepted that having children with people of close relation was not good genetically for the offspring of the couple and the general health of the village. Men found to be lying about indiscretions resulting in pregnancy were punished and shamed for risking bringing disease and a curse onto the community.

The fact there was no recent memory of attack by predator while cooking meant they had all done well in remembering and maintaining village safety measures.

There had been one attack by crocodile and because it was judged as a result of recklessness and disregard for safety it was not counted as an incident that required them to revisit their rules. One area of the river was designated as the source of food, another for bathing. There was a division of bathing areas that kept adults separate from young men and young ladies. On the fateful day of the attack people could recall, a few young boys had gone for a swim, in a part of the river not intended for relaxation. Chanda along with his friends were floating in the water just as they had done several times before, minds at peace, their little bodies cool and enjoying the balance of the heat above and the cold water beneath. He did not see the crocodile coming, he will never know why it chose to attack him and not the others. The first he knew of the attack was when he was pulled under water by the enormous jaws. Upon seeing their friend attacked the other children quickly swam to shore and stood on the stony river beach and watched as Chanda struggled to free himself. In what appeared to be a short fight he had been overpowered and immersed underwater by the creature. Some of the children ran back to call for help, while others remained to keep an eye on what would happen next. Fortunately, in all the flailing, he must have touched what was a weak point and the crocodile suddenly released him, allowing Chanda swam to shore. He did that with what strength he had left after his struggle, he found strength, that up until that point, he never knew he possessed. He had lost his arm as a result, and his face was scarred for life, but he was alive.

Nuclear families and extended tended to share the same compound, ensuring that support systems remained intact and available for family members. The only time a compound freely had happily parted with a member would be on occasions such as weddings, and it was often a young lady being married off to someone from another village or to a man within the village but of another compound. Most men tended to bring their bride home with them, it was unusual but not unheard of that a man moved to his bride's compound.

The diet was primarily pescatarian, bush meat was rarely eaten mainly because of the means required to capture it. People also understood that for the sake of ecological balance, hunting, which normally involved the hunter having to leave the village for days was a restricted means of food, and only done in controlled cycles. There were goat herders among them, cattle farming in Mitondo was rare, chickens roamed freely on the village and some of their eggs were a taken as a source of food. All food was consumed with the importance of balance at the forefront of the community's mind. For the most part, unless there was a wedding or celebration of some sort, excessive animal and bird consumption was not the norm, livestock were generally left alone to graze or to help with farming and as a source of milk. The river was their greatest source of daily food, aside from roots and field produce.

The one incident of attack by predator during the day on the village, happened to be one that would cause a seismic shift in Shikulu's fate and set him on the path he would follow to his final breath.

That afternoon, Shikulu's father Kunda was outside relaxing after a hard day's work when he felt a sudden dread come over him. It was unsettling and persistent enough that he took this as a sign that something was amiss. He decided to inspect the compound first checking for obvious signs of danger to his family. As he walked around searching for the source of unrest in his soul, he noticed the children playing under the warm sun. He observed the women cooking, there were men relaxing and enjoying home brew as they waited for food to be served. He took in the beauty that was the surrounding land of his family's compound. Kunda noticed just as he had before as he sat unwinding at home, how the sun rays fought through the leaves of the enormous surrounding trees, causing the rays to display beautiful leaf and sun patterns on the ground. He felt grateful for the cool breeze that touched his face. Kunda watched as the dust rose in response to the children playing. The more he walked around, the more everything suggested it was a normal day just as many before this day. It was some comfort to him to come to this conclusion, his heart began to settle as his walk around confirmed that everything was as it should be. Despite that assurance he acknowledged that the nudge he had felt was worth looking into later. He decided that he would speak to the spiritual cleanser to sanctify their homes as something was clearly amiss in the spirit realm, or on land and the ancestors had been good enough to warn him.

He was aware some of his family members where not always honorable, only last month one of the uncles had been caught with a married woman from the village, the damages paid, the fighting and unrest among friends that followed, were still lingering in the air. This was even after the Chieftain intervened, Kunda could not bear the thought of another incident so soon after the shameful matter they had just settled. He was sure that whatever the problem in his compound, it was likely to have been caused by one of the men. He would ask the Spiritual cleanser to compel the guilty person to confess and save the compound bad omen or worse tragedy, because of their wrongdoing. Women were rarely the problem, in fact women were such safe vessels of secrets, infertile men in the village remained none the wiser. The culture was designed to save men the embarrassment of knowing they were unable to reproduce. Wives would discreetly have intercourse with a proven fertile man in the community, every village had designated men to fulfil that role. Spiritual women anointed the male who would perform this function, as a rule this route towards conception was only taken by women after having exhausted all other fertility remedies and measures. Men chosen for this important task were known only to the Spiritual cleansers and the woman in need of the service. No woman ever exposed the man who fathered children in their husband's stead. The only time the truth came out, was when one of the chosen men had consumed too much Chibuku (local beer) and decided to brag about his potent semen among the other men. As the other men mocked at him for being drunk and speaking foolishly, his anger compelled him to give the names of the women he had helped impregnate. There was uproar, and from that point on, the privileged person assigned the role of impregnating women, was also bound to live a life free from mind altering substances, especially alcohol in return for all the perks and comforts afforded them. These men were traditionally looked after communally even after they were no longer suitable for the task. No woman, even in anger ever disclosed the truth to their husbands or friends, in this matter and many others they could be trusted. Women were taught to know when a lack of conception had taken long enough to be considered a concern. From the moment they got married, women remained aware of conception time frame.

However, the rules were not as considerate or concerned with discretion when the inability to bear children was wife's condition, especially after having tried all the methods including several meetings with the community stud. In such cases she would be expected to permit her husband to have children with another wife, it was common knowledge that asking the wife was simply a formality. No one really cared whether she agreed or not, it would be done. Whilst this process for the wife was not without contentious moments, children were perceived as being of paramount importance to everyone. Women were expected to make peace with the process. Reflecting on prior incidents within their community, it confirmed Kunda's suspicion that a man had done something impure causing the stir he felt in his spirit. If there was an unclean spirit among them, he was sure it would be because of a man.

Just as he was about to sit back down and enjoy his well-earned rest, at the corner of his eye Kunda saw the grass just behind their house move, then it stopped and moved again, then it stopped again. He wondered what could be making those slow but deliberate movements and by now his instinct for danger had reached peak level. Whatever was making those movements was using the long grass to conceal its identity, his heart had started to race as he watched what he now believed to be an animal stalking something in their compound. Kunda's eyes followed the direction the unknown being was heading and to his horror it was moving towards Kalwe as she was cooking, blissfully unaware of the danger she was in. He ran to his tools and quickly retrieved an axe and almost as if the creature sensed it had been discovered, at that very moment it leapt out of the grass and on to Kalwe. Kunda ran towards his wife with axe in hand, his only thought to free her, because by now she was under the lion screaming.

He swung the axe in the direction of the lion and felt it make firm contact with the back of its mane, he pulled the axe out and swung it and again making contact then pulling his weapon out and plunging it into the lion once more, this time aiming for its head, every skill he possessed as a hunter had come into play, and with his axe he struck the lion again and again. Any hunter will confirm that pulling an axe out of the body of an animal took great skill and strength. On that day Kunda displayed supernatural strength, and he was sure of that, later when his people would examine the lion, they would stand in awe at the wounds he had inflicted onto the animal. In those dangerous seconds, Kunda struck repeatedly and hard enough that it compelled the lion to release Kalwe and turn to him.

There came a point in the fight that every action, every movement became as though he was in a dream. Kunda was aware of the lion raising its paws in his direction but felt nothing. This encouraged him to keep fighting, clearly the ancestors were with him and all the blows the lion landed, felt like nothing. This was a day of good fortune for him, he thought, as the blood on the lion from its injuries revealed to him that the cowardly beast, having chosen to attack his wife was dying with every swing of his axe into its body. Finally, in what felt like a short battle, and the animal having sustained enough wounds fell to its death.

He watched it fall, he watched it die, in that moment Kunda felt like the strongest man on Earth. He had fought a lion, and survived, the feeling of triumph was like nothing he had ever felt. He decided to check on his wife, Kunda imagined she would be in a state of terror after what had happened and he wanted to comfort her, at the same time he imagined how from this day on, songs would be written about him. He was the man who fought a lion to save his wife and had lived to tell the story. But Kunda could not move, his mind had many thoughts of the things he now needed to do, but as he willed his body to move it refused to comply. That is when he saw the razor cuts from the lion's claws all over him, then he saw the blood flowing out of his body. The realisation that he was badly wounded crept up on him slowly, understanding that he was incapable of doing anything to change that gave him enough time to make peace with the transition that would follow. He fell to the ground. Kalwe lay nearby helpless, also badly injured. By the time people had come to their aid, Kunda was dead and Kalwe barely alive. The keepers of stories remained close and listened as she spoke, not all of it made sense, but their job was to listen. She died the following day.

Shikulu never shared the story of how he ended up in the care of Christian missionaries after the death of his parents, there remain no record of how the tragedy in his life led to his separation from the safety of his people and everything he knew as a support system in their community. His people remain in the dark as to whether he chose to leave because he saw an opportunity to explore or if he was simply taken, they (missionaries) did that sometimes. If they had to guess, using what information they had on him, it was a strategic move on his part to withhold information that would distract from the direction he wanted them to keep focus on. He focused on the narrative that presented him as strong, always in control and a master visionary. He needed them to believe this not only because he wanted them to follow his instruction but also because he needed them to trust in his leadership. The sad truth is a cost maintaining his story of being all knowing also involved, denying the existence of his moments of vulnerability. The erasure of a scared orphan and any grieving that may have taken place in his life, invariably took away from the richness of his life's journey.

There is no timeline given of the period he spent among people with warped views of spirituality and an unearned sense of superiority over other humans. Everything they know about Shikulu was what he wanted to be remembered, therefore what remains in memory up to this point is of a man who planned everything, nothing surprised him. He often mentioned that surprises were merely unique moments given to us to learn from and adjust and if anyone was a master of adjusting and evolving it was him.

The story of young man once destined to be a Mwata (Head Chief) who found himself in the care of missionaries, the Puritans no less will forever remain untold. As for the Puritans they had no personal interest in him, his history or what was expected of him in any matters not of their religion. Their mission was to save souls, and unless your history was European you were unclean, this often meant the Black Africans and others with Brown skin. Our songs or stories were irrelevant to them.

For Puritans, conversion of those with Black skin was the greatest of achievements, a noble cause no less, each conversion was a story to share with others like them. On a personal level they imagined their commitment to their word, would ensure a higher place in the next life. The people of faith in that time would also ironically play a pivotal role in being one the greatest destructive forces to our people's culture, and to others whom they would encounter in the world. That was not a matter that concerned them even after the fact. They slept well assured that spreading their message was greater than worldly peace, kindness, understanding or simply recognise another person's humanity. If they had to, they would inflict pain till skin ripped off the bodies of any targeted individuals, to get their message of faith and love across to the Africans. They believed in their call to save the impure, and with every beating, even death they felt spiritually elevated. Their god was needed by all and would be accepted by everyone, the blood, pain, death and tears of Africans were merely confirmation of the importance of their work.

They were cruel and they were evangelical in their mission to save souls, refusing to accept this path became an opportunity for correction in the denier, they were feared, and governments dare not challenge their madness.

What was never openly discussed was without exception all of them, preachers, mercenaries, invaders, every single one of them was motivated to occupy the continent primarily because of how much money could be made from the "new" to them land. When all was said and done money was the driving force in their presence there. Introducing civilisation and education was the acceptable cloak they used to cover their true intent. They told themselves other stories to explain and justify their presence in the new land, but the truth though unspoken remained clear.

Missionaries being the supervisors of morality insisted that for them souls came first, the vast wealth was merely reward from their god as form of acknowledgement and assistance in furtherance of their necessary work. The converted people often wondered if any of missionaries saw themselves as the indigenous people did? To many they were the earthly representation of evil, the forcibly converted remained unsure if the Puritans themselves had ever believed the words they forced fed others. Had they cared to find out, they would have discovered that our people followed different spiritual rules, not less than just different. They would have learned that to our people, those among us who practiced harmful acts were less likely to delude themselves into believing it was for a greater good. Yes, we had wars, and some among us indulged in the aspect of medicine or spirituality that was harmful to others, our societies had witnessed the ugly side of humanity without the help of external forces. But the denial that the invaders walked in was puzzling for our people.

They taught Shikulu what they believed to be civilised living which included their education system. Not one of them asked how the Indigenous people counted, there was no particular interest in the native communication system beyond what they needed to be conveyed, this remained the case during and after their arrival. As far as they were concerned their way was supreme and others irrelevant. As for respecting our people as human beings or even equals, the very idea was out of the question. Then men and women of faith were not opposed to slavery; any good believer knows that if you comb through the good book long enough, you will find justification any heinous behavior. Slavery provided much needed wealth, this ethical and theological quandary was resolved very quickly by rationalising that salvation had given the African something more valuable than worldly desires, and peace on Earth was not a necessity for them after salvation as a result. Missionaries comfort in those thoughts, giving them confidence that their duty had been met.

The final act was to make the Africans accomplices in their abuse, this was done by feeding Africans a daily diet of acceptance that life was pain and inferiority was the nature of humility. Assurances were given that all who endured without complaint would be rewarded by their king in the next life. The fact that this world was not for its occupants (Africans) to find rest and solace was drummed in, and emphasis placed on peace and riches to come in the afterlife. Scriptures of streets paved with gold upon death were reinforced by missionaries, until the converted accepted that joy on earth was meaningless in comparison. For souls that were being beaten down, to point the body could no longer feel, as their eyes watched everything, they held dear being torn apart. Stories of life with sweet music accompanying every step taken on streets paved with gold, became a lifeline and offered hope where there was none. This justification was useful especially when acts of brutality were given. Had they bothered to check they would have noticed that the Africans had seen the many contradictions in what the invaders and people of faith said and what they did. Their god said we were all equal on earth, yet the same people sharing that gift of salvation were facilitating inequality. They took the silence and dismay of the Africans as acceptance and consent.

They kept incorrect interpretations of our lives, ways and habits, fortunately missing the knowledge that, we kept silent when the goal was to allow another to believe they had the upper hand, while we planned what to do. Then when the time was right, we would act. the people understood very well the vanity of feeling better than, and how it followed a pattern of blinding the prideful to the truth of reality. We keep silent, we stored our beliefs somewhere safe within us and waited for the right time to release the truth of who we are.

Not everyone found silence easy, many were exhausted by the relentless cruelty in the guests they had welcomed. Their insatiable hunger to oversee hell over others was unlike anyone in that time had witnessed. Many chose to convert, if only to live what was left of their lives in peace. Ancestors had shared stories of torment before, which provided much needed assurance that all horror passed soon enough, but they had never described anything like these new people. Our people were aware that evil and its reign was often cyclical so even if peace from this hell would not happen in their lifetime it would come eventually. They trusted that balance would force its will on the world as they had witnessed it done before.

One afternoon during his time with the missionaries, without warning Shikulu was informed that he was at an age where he was required to go and fight in the war abroad. His costs would be covered, and his physical needs such as food would be met; the reasons why, were not for him to know at that point, and he was advised that when he arrived in England, he would be given further instructions on what was required of him. By the time he was being informed of his impeding journey everything had been decided for him and there was no room to, ask, refuse or even contemplate, just like that he was on his way to a foreign land.

When Shikulu returned from the Great war he was convinced even more than before, after having lived among them that the imperialists were forever a destructive presence, they could not be trusted and because we had given them a chance to gain a foot hold in our land, he feared extraction would be difficult if not properly thought through. His ultimate fear was that after they left, we would remain their slaves in some form or another. Having lived among them during the war he had witnessed that they were people whose word meant nothing, people who treated their own kind of a certain status as disposable. But the greatest concern was his discovery that they never left any land they sunk their teeth into without taking much more than the Indigenous people ever realised could be taken by an invading force. He saw that they operated much like the one the puritanical missionaries called the deceiver.

When he returned home, he refused to be broken by what he had seen, even the memories of his young body lying under dead bodies while the other army walked over them, could deter him from what he needed to do. Shikulu had decided that what he had seen was enough to commit his remaining days fighting to save his people, he resolved to accept a life of insufficient rest if that was what he needed to do to fulfil his goal. Like many of his people he held the belief that when he transitioned to join the ancestors, he would get his well-earned rest then. This may have also been his way of making sense of and coping with the brutality he had witness in his short life.

He kept his head down and began to follow the steps, he had set in his mind and heart as the path to achieving his ultimate vision. Shikulu excelled in their education system, and they marveled at his intellect, though their praise was that of an adult observing a child perform functions above their developmental stages. He welcomed this condescension, every moment they underestimated him gave him much needed advantage. He never showed them the truth in his heart, he had a plan, that he knew would save his people. He sailed through their education system and seeing that for him the sky was the limit they asked him what direction he wished to take for a career.

Cultural Differences

He chose teaching, the skill of conveying a message effectively was integral to his plan and he executed that role long and efficiently enough to win the trust of the ever-changing nameless invaders. They eventually decided that he was their chosen native Headmaster. The truth was the rural locations were harsh on the invaders and they had convinced themselves that they could not be expected to be everywhere. They never admitted to finding the rural areas in the country inexplicably dark, and for reasons they dare not say out loud, they came to the decision that rural areas were best suited to native people. Therefore, recruiting Indigenous people to continue the good work they established seemed like the next logical step. They never admitted the fact that rural areas often felt impenetrable to their religion and rural inhabitants tended to hold on to their beliefs more so than those that lived in the urban areas. All attempts to rid them of what the invaders called evil spirits had failed. The sheer number of believers of the old ways was overwhelming, so much so that even the land itself appeared to refuse to be separated from that spiritual energy.

There was a spiritual resistance to their presence that left the invaders in a constant state of unease, added to the fact that from time to time there would be a look from one of the villagers, a curse uttered coupled with unexpected and menacing fogs that perpetuated the constant threat of imminent danger. This fear coupled with lack of proper sleep, were among a number of reasons that compelled the new arrivals to move along swiftly from rural areas. Stories of dark practices by Africans were a major crowd puller when they returned home, in their versions the natives were primitive and of course the story tellers the brave saviors. None ever admitted to living in total fear throughout their time, in what they referred to as the dark areas, nor did they share the fact that, they all had a story of that one time a spiritual doctor, told them that what had been put on them for their evil could never be lifted.

Whilst rural areas of the country were perceived as a test of character and bravery for the imperialists. All failed to acclimate very well to their surroundings, especially their women, who mostly chose to flee preferring urban areas that had been interfered with to appear more like their homeland. These changes were introduced in the name of civilisation for those in need of it. Recruiting natives to continue their work also freed them to turn their focus onto the important task of monetising the newly discovered lands. For some this was done in the name of queen and country. They deliberately used language presenting them in a flattering and superior light and not the same for the Indigenous people. Therefore, making claims to have discovered a land gave the undiscerning listener the impression that before the invaders there was nothing. Though the people found their thinking peculiar, the message had begun to infiltrate in many minds and was slowly changing them. It was getting harder to retain their sense of self and as a result many were lost to this new reality. What they would never have foreseen were the generations that would be affected by this poison.

But Shikulu had a plan to stop the damage in its tracks.

First, he would become Headmaster to use their weapon to educate our people about them, in the hope that the next generation would have a better understanding of how to resist and dislodge them. He believed that if the people of his time planned and executed things well enough, the next generation would oversee the return of our stories from the shadows and be wiser having successfully retained our customs and added to them new knowledge of other worlds. He knew enough not share all the details of his vison with everyone and kept all futuristic information and time frames close to his heart, he was intent on approaching liberation one step at a time. Having a clear map to liberation outlined by him and known only to him was also a form of control for Shikulu, he would assess his strategies regularly for potential problems and make adjustments were necessary. Shikulu knew that everyone without exception would need to participate in the struggle for true freedom. Because of that he decided to begin by educating both the boys and the girls in understanding the invaders, this was at a time when girls were not afforded the same educational opportunities primarily in rural areas. He knew that convincing the village and the chieftain to prepare the boys for future freedom fighting would be an easy sell. But he needed everyone, men, women, boys and girls for us to not only move forward in a focused way, but to be able to effectively undermine and dismantle the new system. The girls more so than the women would need to be immersed in the western form of education just as the boys were being made to do so. He was aware asking that of girls would be a challenge, the continuation of life was a sacred act, and interfering with the important role that girls near to or of conception age played within society or any woman's ability to continue life on earth for that matter was taboo. Even at our people's worst times during war, only a select group of women were chosen to fight, the majority were protected and trained to do all that they could to save themselves and continue life.

This new type of education would mean less focus for the girls and their families on finding the right future partner, less concern with honing the skills necessary for preparing homes for the next generation and directing focus on freeing us from the immediate threat instead. In his plan, Shikulu believed this was necessary procreation disruption, to facilitate a return to life closer to what we had before. The way they learned was another peculiarity, that our people had observed about them. In their world learning had a peak, in our land the people were in a constant state of learning until they moved on to the next life. The idea that one had to suspend all living and focus only on learning was an alien concept, because in our land living and learning were one. In any case Headmaster wanted all the young children trained to understand how the imperialists educated themselves, Shikulu also understood and accepted that later full-on combat would need to be integrated in the plan to rid themselves of this alien presence. They needed to prepare while the imperialists remained assured that they were asleep.

The village was big, and Shikulu remembered his mother's influence on their family, he thought a lot about how this was true for every compound and decided it would be shrewd to begin with talking to the women in the village about his vision for girls first. Mother was god to them and he was right to begin there; mother had been placed on an almost supernatural pedestal by them. But sadly, this also meant if a mother was assessed as behaving in a way that was perceived to be beneath her high standing, there would be a permanent stain on her entire household. Husbands and children were immune to the heavy burden of being the single cause of such a mark on the whole family. In fact, when bad behavior was witnessed in husbands or children it would often be ascribed to the lack of stability and order from the core of the family which was always mother. They were several sayings for households of fallen mothers, one was a quick reference to the unfairness of expecting a child to have sense where the mother did not and many such unforgiving tales to remind women and girls that mistakes were not their privilege to make. Mothers were literally and figuratively the symbols of life; they were also entrusted with everyone's memory through story and song to be passed on to the next generation.

For all his intellect, Shikulu lacked proper understanding of community etiquette, mostly because his upbringing among his people had been temporarily disrupted. The women in the community knew that and made allowance for his frequent clumsy approaches to almost all things within their society. He was not aware of this personality short coming, and his internalised western arrogance meant he assumed that how he presented himself was always seen through a lens of reverence and respect for his immense knowledge and worldly experience. They never told him the truth because they chose to see and prioritise his intentions for them as being mostly good, over his frequent missteps. Plus, many of the women liked the idea of their daughters gaining new knowledge, the new ways would be of benefit to the next generation, and the women were easily persuaded into accepting Headmaster's vision.

Shikulu was married to Lupapa, also called mama (grandmother), he was much older than Lupapa when they married, however, this was not unusual for the time if anything this was the accepted norm. Lupapa was his second wife. Before her, Shikulu had been married to the catch of the village. When he returned from war, and the Puritans eventually moved along leaving him behind, he successfully located the place his people had been instructed to remain, many remembered his grandfather Yoram, enough people remembered his people and they quickly embraced him. They gave him a piece of land on the village to begin his compound. Most of his siblings had moved back to the Congo to be nearer their father's people which meant he was alone and because of this the Elders recommended that he marry. As was tradition they found a potential wife for him, she was beautiful, and her name was Chisala. For her the chance to be married to a man so well-travelled, who spoke many languages, was too good an opportunity to decline. Besides, she was beautiful, everyone said so and beautiful girls married successful men. She knew that a man with such an interesting story needed a beautiful first wife and though she would discover later that his faith meant she would be his only wife, that did not bother her as she still felt happy with the thought of being a great man's one and only.

Chisala learned soon enough that Shikulu, had rigid ways, she found him strange especially his fixation on the minutia. Things most would consider inconsequential being out of place would make him deeply unhappy. Which would be fine except there were occasions he would refuse to eat because she had not stored the food in his exact prescribed way, when he got home from work. The shock of being told that how she was raised to feed her family was not of a high standard enough for him was offensive to Chisala. It was also insulting to those that had taught her. Before they got married, she had been told what he liked to eat as well as what his people in general ate. The type of home he wanted to have, was also part of the information she was given, she was familiarised on all matters concerning him and what he enjoyed before they got married. However, no one could have prepared her for his unique characteristics. Her people been honest with his people about who she was including her needs and wants. Consequently, Chisala felt cheated to find out important information about the man who was now her husband after all had been said and done. In no time, she became unhappy in her marriage.

There was the house cleaning routine or rather regime, he insisted on very specific cleaning methods, the house had to be pristine in a way that was by any one's standards oppressive. She had never known him to do any cleaning, but he insisted on living in a highly sanitised environment. He also saw fit to hand out unsolicited instructions on every task assigned to the wife in their community.

He insisted Chisala embrace western education, as he felt strongly that the community needed to see order into his home first. She did not want that life, she wanted to think about having children, meeting other women in the field and all that went along with being a married woman in Mitondo. Of course, she looked forward to talking about marriage to such an accomplished man with her other married sisters. The whole point of her family accepting his request for marriage, was that she continued life as they knew it. At no point did she conceive even in her wildest imagination that marriage would involve studying the ways of a new land and implementing them in her home. She was beautiful, men in the village had fought for her, this was not the way men treated beautiful wives. As for intimacy, she allowed the other women to tease her about how joyful the experience must be, how could she add to that? She did not know what ecstasy was.

Chisala with the smile that raised the pulses of both men and pubescent boys, a woman so breath-takingly beautiful that she had to be protected from all males in the village, yet here she was desperately unhappy being married to Shikulu. He was not enamored with her beauty, which was his first offense in her mind. This knowledge started taking its toll on her feeling of self-worth, she believed that every time he looked at her, he saw someone that needed improving. Sometimes she would tell herself that if that is what he believed he was a mad man, there was not a part of her that needed improving as far as she was concerned, in fact people had told her as much. But knowing this was not enough to keep her confidence intact. She knew that if she wanted to live, she would have to leave before all of her died in that loveless big colonial building, that he had been given to oversee.

Then she remembered Abonge, a warrior, strong, muscular, big in stature, and she wanted him. In fact, before Shikulu's people spoke to hers, she had chosen Abonge and she knew that he wanted her too. Abonge was the type of man she understood, and she was confident he knew how a woman of her caliber expected to be treated. She felt sure that he would not need to be taught how to care for her, she knew this even without ever having been with him. Chisala also knew in her heart that he would know how to love her body. Before Shikulu arrived, everyone was sure that Abonge and Chisala were a match, before headmaster their union was as good as decided. If only she had spoken up in his defense on the day Headmaster's proposal was announced to her people. If only she had brought up Abonge's achievements among her people and how good he was with guiding the young men in the community, maybe life would be different for her now. But Headmaster sounded like the better choice to her at the time as well and everyone else including her parents, who felt it was the right and clever thing to do. When her family were officially notified of Shikulu's intention to marry their daughter they took the chance to steer their family in a new and exciting direction.

All of Shikulu's focus was on the school and ensuring the teaching was being applied at a standard he felt acceptable. When he came home, it seemed to Chisala that whatever she did, he remained distracted and unhappy, she found him and his vision tiresome. One morning something came over her and she decided that more than anything she wanted to feel the way Abonge made her feel again. She started by planning her days to include moments she could meet him as they both carried out their daily work. She diverted from her regular route to fetch water, using one that she was sure would lead to an encounter with Abonge. She was the first to engage in flirtatious talk and he did not resist, he loved her. This carried on for weeks and Abonge began to live for their close but sadly distant encounters. On the days he missed seeing her he would wait until he was sure she was not coming round, before carrying on with his day. He did that every time they missed each other. She attended all weekly community gatherings, every celebration, whether it was to mark a successful harvest, a wedding or a new life joining them, she attended them all to make sure she saw Abonge. Those days spent speaking to Abonge injected life back into her soul. Shikulu full of puritan thoughts and busy with training found social gatherings a waste of valuable time, especially when planning and resting needed to be done. He never attended any of the festivities.

She was glad for this gift from all things holy, it gave her a chance to catch Abonge's dark eyes, she never needed to check if he watched as she walked near him, she knew that he watched her every move. When she was alone with the other wives they would tell mention, how Abonge would go into a trance whenever he saw her, they found it funny that he could not keep his eyes off her, deep down she loved those inappropriate conversations and feared that it was not just Abonge who was beginning to give himself away. She was falling further and further away from Shikulu and toward Abonge it was only a matter of time that they would both be found out, if people had not already begun to guess. At night she worried that he would be married off, but then she would speak to him during the day and be reassured that he was meant to be with her and would never accept another woman. The nights she thought of losing Abonge kept her up with sadness and after one such distressing night, she made a very important decision.

She wanted him and he wanted her, why not make their love complete? Who would know that she had been with him? Maybe that was the thing that would free them both, she knew she was lying to herself, but she needed that lie to do what she wanted to do. After another of Shikulu's dissatisfied days she decided not to bother waiting for the right time. She knew where Abonge would be, she knew that sex with him would open her soul and allow more room for him in her life. There was no fear or worry left, all concerns that others might find out what was really in her heart dissipated. Chisala had heard the other wives talking about occasions when women who lacked fulfilment in their marriages sought the company of other men to meet needs not being met by their husbands. There were men so skilled in the art of pleasing a woman that they made women burn with such desire and ecstasy they could not breathe or think, after the encounters with their lovers those women returned home to their husbands happier and repeated that cycle over and over until they reached an age their sexual fulfilment was no longer a necessity. No one suggested Chisala do that, the wives were merely sharing what they had heard other women do in certain situations, but as far as Chisala was concerned they were speaking directly to her heart.

She was so bored with Shikulu she had not even bothered to use the training all women in the village were given to ensure maximum enjoyment and pleasure for husband and wife during sex. What was the point, he was hardly interested. Those puritans had taken that aspect of his manhood away and sex was a function rather than what other women had promised her would become a like drug that would make her to crawl back to her husband and beg for more, in the privacy of their home of course. The wives told her that it tasted so good she would forgive him almost anything.

She wanted that feeling, she needed the heat that could only come from merging her body with Abonge's. She decided to speak freely to Abonge about how she felt, it was time to go beyond flirtation, she dispensed with all pretense and politeness and decided to escalate the current stalemate. Chisala wanted Abonge to hear the sexual intentions she had for him. She followed him to the one place that would make clear how she really felt. He was working in what was a scared place for everyone; the rules were clear, and they were maintained based on trust. To everyone's knowledge no woman had ever violated that space until the day Chisala decided that showing up there was the only way to convey to Abonge how strongly she felt.

Abonge as one of the older men was required from time to time to help with the training of pubescent boys as they went through their rite of passage. She followed him on the long trek to the discreet designated place where training relating to matters concerning puberty and manhood took place. She knew what this place meant for her people. Only male teachers trained and anointed were allowed in that place. But this was also the safest place she could think of to be alone with him, despite knowing that her presence there was a desecration of a sacred site. But she also trusted that taking the risk to permanently stain the rituals of all the young men attending would make the men think twice before admitting to seeing her at the site. She waited until the time was right, Chisala watched as the young men having been put through a grueling day were finally sent on personal tasks reducing the number of possible witnesses on site before showing herself.

Ukume saw her, he knew this was forbidden, he knew it was wrong. One day he would marry and would not want this to happen to him nor would he want his son's sacred transition interfered with in this unclean way. On the other hand, Abonge was a good friend, and Ukume understood more than anyone that Abongo was willing to start unrest like no other over Chisala. Ukume being a man took only a short time to reflect, he found himself taking comfort in the knowledge that men did this sort of thing all the time. He had been told stories of such uncontrollable sexual urges between two people that they were compelled to be together physically by forces out of their control. He rationalised that in the scheme of things allowing the two to meet in this way was the wise decision. Flames can only grow and burn for so long. Why destroy the lives of young men over a matter so easily resolved? Ukume pretended not to see her even though she knew he had, he looked down when Abonge looked at him to check if he would object. Ukume's assessment had been correct. Abonge had been burning for Chisala for so long, the fight that would have ensued had his brother objected to him being with her would have been the wounding and potentially the death of one if not both of them.

Once Abonge saw her, he knew immediately what it meant, he walked to her his feet getting heavier with every step, every part of him knew that there would be no turning back after this point. He reminded himself that all he cared about was her, then the thought of being with her quickened his pace and before he knew it, he had fallen into her arms, with equal speed he ushered her to a part of the woods that was discreet. There was not much to take off her body, the wrap she had on fell off with ease and for the first time Chisala understood the joy that was having a man inside of her. The completion that she felt with him was what she had been promised was the point of marriage. Just like that all the traditional sexual training she had been given by the women in the village came into effect. Everything came together with Abonge, this was what love was supposed to feel like and she cried because her life with Shikulu was not like this, she did not want to leave the man that she loved, a man who clearly loved her back, to return to a place void of love.

For months they met and merged souls while exchanging bodily fluids, when she fell pregnant and knowing it could not be anyone but Abonge's, she met with the medicine woman who gave her a root to soak in a jar of water for ten days then drink. That solved her immediate problem and she continued to meet Abonge for sex and love. Shikulu was so oblivious to what was happening in his home and about women in general that he never noticed a change in his wife or that they had not had sex in months.

One day after another of their numerous passionate encounters Abonge decided it was enough and she needed to make a choice. It was the easiest ultimatum she had ever been given because by then she was prepared to die for him. Chisala was even prepared to be universally shamed for him. But for the sake of her immediate and extended family, she decided to take the traditional route to end her marriage. She met with an aunty that she trusted and told her the truth, Chisala needed someone she could be honest with so that they could help her effectively. Each family protected their own members. When her aunty advised her that many in the village already found Shikulu with his western education insufferable. It gave Chisala comfort, her aunty told her that she would push for separation that would be easy, and her niece's honour would remain intact. She asked Chisala to hold off on declaring her encounters with Abonge to others, promising her that it was not to diminish what the two lovers felt, but rather that they had to be clever from that point on.

Aunty explained to Chisala that tradition was what would save her, and according to their tradition for the first year a bride's younger sibling was required to live with the newlyweds, for the specific purpose of observing the husband to make sure he was not abusive, and his new wife was safe with him. Since most newlywed wives were judged as being too excited about marriage to pay attention to warnings signs, the sibling who loved her was there to be the eyes her married sister needed. Chisala's young sister Mwenya, according to tradition had accompanied her into her marital home.

Aunty said: "First let us begin by hearing what your sister has to say of the months she has lived with you and your husband".

Aunty advised against disclosing to her sister any information regarding Abonge and fortunately her sister was none the wiser to what Chisala had been up to, and provided her account of their marriage was negative, Chisala had a chance to leave Shikulu with her dignity.

After Aunty had spoken to Chisala, she went on to share with the other relevant female Elders the news of Chisala's intention to leave Headmaster. She informed them that Chisala had chosen her as designated advocate. It was then decided that along with the other selected female elders in the compound, that an official meeting would be set, to speak with Chisala's sister, everyone was advised not to let Mwenya catch wind of the impending meeting. The thinking being if she was not prepared, she would not have time to make up a lie to protect her sister, the community worked on a principle of trust so the idea that Chisala would corrupt the role of the one sent to protect her was unthinkable. As planned, Mwenya was summoned on the agreed date and time without warning.

Because all things holy is good Mwenya's verbal report depicted a sad regimented marriage unlike anything in our culture. She described Headmaster as unreasonable, unyielding and stuck in his routines, even worse she called him and his home joyless. Mwenya recounted how his unloving nature to her sister coupled with his obsession with the new religion had begun to strip the life out of Chisala. She told them of evening meals would often be eaten cold because Headmaster prayed over them for long stretches at a time, then prayers would follow after dinner and before going to sleep. Guests were known to fall asleep during many of his long prayer sessions. It was not unknown for some to murmur under their breath while others were content with rolling their eyes during prayers. Mwenya explained how Headmaster rarely took time to spend with Chisala, and it was no surprise to her that her sister was still not pregnant. From what she had observed her sister was sad all the time, and Mwenya feared Chisala's marriage to Headmaster was destroying everything that was alive in her. She described the disturbing and constant correction her sister endured and by the time she was done, the Elders sat alarmed. They questioned Chisala if she had tried speaking to her husband about his behaviour, she replied that he treated her more like a child than his wife, never taking into consideration what she had to say even about the household. Between the two sisters the life they described was very sad.

The Elder women conveyed this message to the male Elders, who insisted on compelling Chisala to try harder, but as the aunties expected, she declined, she wanted the marriage to end. A meeting under the village Baobab tree was called. All the elders from both families were present that day, Headmaster was present with his advocates as were Chisala and Mwenya. The tree they sat under was significant as it was the chosen place for discussions of such magnitude. Headmaster had people speaking for him as he sat in silence having given them his version of events. Chisala had her people speaking for her and so the day was a back-and-forth account of each person's defence and explanations.

Headmaster was at a disadvantage because the couple had no children, that would be seen as a failure on his part, and he knew that it could make parting easier. But he had asked his representatives to fight with all they knew to save his marriage, because as much as he was committed to fighting the imperialists, their indoctrination also lived within him. Therefore, without even acknowledging it, deep within him lay a debilitating fear of divorce. As far as he was concerned their union had to be preserved. No one in the community took divorce lightly but to them humans had to be willing to stay together.

Elder witness after witness came and spoke for and against either husband or wife, proverbs were used to make points, reminders that marriage was sacred were made. By the end of the day, it became apparent to Chisala that she would be compelled to return to Shikulu for one more try and as this reality became more evident Chisala decided she would rather die than spend another day in the shadows with Abonge, with that thought in mind just before they could disperse for the day, Chisala with momentum and a voice she did not recognise stood up and declared that she loved Abonge and he loved her. The shock of this revelation necessitated the need for everyone to go back to their homes, to talk and reflect on the fuller picture that they now had. It was also an opportunity to speak to Shikulu to find out if he still wanted to save his marriage after his wife's declaration. Everyone needed time to allow what they had learned from their ancestors to show them the right way to proceed in this matter. Abonge would also need be spoken to, this could only be done with his people present.

Having carried in his heart and chest, his wife's confession at the meeting, before they had even arrived home Shikulu advised his people to let her people know that she was free to leave. He did not want a prisoner in his home, he knew from experience what that reality meant. Whilst he was not a passionate man in marriage, he wanted a woman who wanted to be with him. On a practical level when word got round about Abonge it would distract from his work, it was better to let her go in a way that was as peaceful as possible. His people returned to convey his wishes the same night and just as Shikulu had instructed, his wife's people were informed and Chisala was free.

The Elders came to visit him after enough moons had passed and advised that if he wanted to engage the people in his future plans, he would have to remarry, a man his age being single was not our way and would cause people to worry and wonder about him. Shikulu having been quietly devastated by the end of his first marriage insisted that he was too busy to take time tending to a needy wife. The Elders agreed that a giant thorn in your foot was better than an unhappy home. They proceeded to assure him that they had learned from what had transpired with his first wife and believed they had found the right person for him this time round.

They told him about Lupapa, how intelligent she was, but importantly that she picked new ideas up very quickly. They shared how she had learned to knit, to make cultural medicines and was a talented midwife having added to her child birthing knowledge from women in the village, with training she had obtained from Belgian nurses. She was 17 at that point, which made her achievements very impressive. Shikulu was concerned by her age because he was in his thirties. But it was explained to him that she was mature over what her age suggested. They told him how she had been practically supporting her entire compound since her father passed away. They added that her eagerness to learn and operate in excellence was what made her the perfect wife for him. They explained how she could work alongside him, halving his load and importantly he would regain the respectability that came with marriage in their community

They suggested that before deciding, he go over to her compound, to meet her, and watch her work as she practiced midwifery from her family compound. Her skills in her vocation had been perfected to the point that the only women she sent to hospital were those she assessed to be experiencing complications beyond her abilities. She had been trained to identify antenatal problems at an early stage, and she also had an instinct for how to approach each expectant woman in her care, respecting that each pregnancy was unique, because of her approach many women preferred her intervention to that of the nuns. Understanding customs whilst providing a service that required trust was what also made her invaluable to the community, she was so trusted that the women, she referred to the hospital would often cry and insist she attempt to help them.

Lupapa later known as Mama (Grandmother) was remembered as being physically strong, her life had been dedicated to self-improvement, personal growth and she exuded knowledge. When her people were approached about a possible marriage with Headmaster, she could not believe her luck, as far as she was concerned, she was getting the best of all worlds. First the marriage would be a chance to exchange and share love with a man, and an opportunity at starting her own family with the added benefit of being in an educational environment because of her current suitor. There were many conversations between the families. But she was always going to say yes. Like him she was of the same faith but a different denomination. Small adjustments that she was willing to make. Later they would observe that their marriage was not explosive with passion nor was it dramatic, instead it was serene and because of their faith they took this as a sign that their union had the approval and presence of God.

The groom's people began by going to the bride-to-be's home with a variety of food that he enjoyed eating. Aside from familiarising her with what his people enjoyed eating. This practise was also in place because she would be the primary person making or overseeing the cooking in their home, therefore she would need to know what food was his favourite to please him. This was also then done in reverse and her people brought along with them to the meeting food that best represented their homes and traditions. For the man the idea was that he would provide the food she loved as a sign of his love for her. Normally an animal or more would have been killed and cooked for such an occasion, but Shikulu resisted all grand gestures, he was also strongly opposed to the consumption of alcohol or any mind-altering substance and since he knew that wedding festivities would invariably have Chibuku, he made his intention for an alcohol-free celebration known through his spokesperson. This aversion to alcohol consumption is something he had, reiterated to everyone in conversation especially to the pupils in school and later in life when he had his own children. The dangers of alcohol and how he had personally witnessed many people's lives destroyed by its consumption was another mission he felt he had to embark upon with passion.

There was no natural way for his family and guests to celebrate the precursor to his marriage without Chibuku and other alcoholic substances so from that point on everything felt askew. Shaking their heads at the strangeness of the man they represented, his people conveyed his wishes for a small celebration with no alcohol. They also cancelled the standard party plans that would have included most of the people in the village. Shikulu brought gifts for Lupapa's mother and because her father was with the ancestors, he gave Lupapa's eldest paternal uncle, all gifts intended for the father of a bride-to-be. He met with the women he would need to speak with in the event he had issues with Lupapa, and in the same way she met with his people. In his mind and heart, Shikulu told himself that this time he was going to do things differently, except for the party rituals of course, nothing could make him attend a function with alcohol being served. But this time he promised to see and hear his wife if only to avoid the shame of losing love to neglect.

The night before her wedding day she met with the women of the village and they taught her what marriage was and the bedroom dance, it is literally a dance performed during sex. They explained how to position yourself for each sexual organ size to maximise pleasure so that in any eventuality the woman would know what to do. Being part of the group of natural remedy women, she already knew where the fertility roots could be found, as well as medication for simple health issues such as headaches, stomachache or libido enhancement. She knew were to source the root sap that could be used before and after labor to help the new mother's body fall back into place, heal and continue to function well. The wedding night and future days as woman and mother were a full course taught before she began her role in her new and natural direction.

The men also met the night before and were supposed to share knowledge according to culture and tradition, conversations for them would revolve around challenges men encountered during marriage and what methods or actions they took to overcame problems. Some discussed where other men fell in marriage, and those that were in that position shared the pitfalls that came with having more than one wife. Sex being a part of marriage is also touched upon though the intensive teaching in men was done in greater depth during their rite of passage. However, between Shikulu failing to make real friendships among the men, and the fact they had given up trying to bond with him culturally, many where unwilling to be candid on his night. A few of them were also still annoyed that he had cancelled the chance for a wedding party preferring something more sedate and infuriatingly he had also banned Chibuku and all forms of alcohol on his final night. As was the case with his first marriage no one shared any wisdom of substance with him.

Shikulu knew how they felt about him, and one of the things he liked about Lupapa was how well she interacted with people. He wondered if maybe after they got married, he could learn from her how to best approach others traditionally. He toyed with the idea that maybe he could leave the handling of people to her entirely. This thought was soon overtaken by his pride and lack of acceptance that he needed to change anything about himself. He believed that it was important for him to assert his authority otherwise people soon fell into over familiarity and disorder. He quickly convinced himself that his way was best, and the community would have to change instead. After all, he was hardly doing all this for himself, there was a bigger picture and they needed to understand that.

When all traditional customs had been followed, Lupapa (Mama) was sent home with Shikulu a married woman.

His idiosyncrasies were not an issue with her as what she was known for was assimilating and learning. Having learned from his past mistakes Shikulu was more open to having a wife with her own voice and dreams. As his home was now in order he could focus on the school and executing his educational plan. Mama soon began a routine of waking up before many awoke in the community, to begin preparations for Shikulu's day, in the way he had told her he preferred. She did everything, including preparing his breakfast which would be ready by the time she had heated his bath water. This organisation ensured she could also carry on supporting the women medically and teaching the young girls to sew, knit and for a select few, training to understand how we produced local medicine. When she fell pregnant it was as though everything was coming together for the two of them. Mama worked so hard people wondered when she rested. Her home became a prominent place where others went to eat after work. Guests choosing your home for a meal was an honour in this environment and before long, Mama had learned to cook for many on a regular basis. Food was eaten by hand and served on massive communal clay plates, everyone sat around these plates and ate together.

When it came time to have her baby, two female mid wives came to her home, to assist with the delivery. As soon as the baby was delivered the women wrapped Lupapa's mid-section tight with Chitenge (traditional wrap) and as was tradition she was taken to the river were all three women sat in the water and the new mother would be given a specific full body massage of the muscles with special emphasis around her tummy area, this would be followed by a hot water and cloth massage the next day. The process of body massages was repeated for a whole month. Having lost women to bleeding after birth in the past, experienced woman in the community would attend to new mothers for after birth care, which would take up to a month. In that time the new mum's body would be inspected to check among other things that the after-birth blood flow was normal. Despite being a mid-wife as well Mama had to be tended to the same as every other mother after delivering a baby. This care was given however many children the mother had conceived prior to a current birth. The entire process including birth remedies, that will have already been soaking in the water for a designated time frame, would be administered till the after-birth midwives were satisfied that the new mother was well enough to carry on without them. New Mothers recovered better when they were looked after in this way. Those who later did not live near rivers continued this traditional care with their daughters as way of keeping their voices alive

By the time Mama had 4 children many of the community's children were attending lessons at Headmasters school. Shikulu was setting apart children that were natural teachers to help elevate their peers who were struggling especially with learning foreign languages.

Creative Differences

Grace was one of his talented pupils, it would not be an exaggeration to say she was the most talented of his pupils. She embodied everything Shikulu was trying to show his people about what could be achieved if the girls were included in future plans to free our people. Later when he was older and dying from cancer, he shared with his daughter his fears that even in success, those imperialists had changed us irreversibly. However, before then he had been hopeful, even inspired by the developments being made at the school. He had long decided that for his plan to been seen to have any integrity, his home had to be the perfect representation of his expectations at work. As a result, even when school days were over, they continued for his children at home. Mumba was Shikulu and Mama's first born, he was undeniably his father's pride and joy. Mumba being the first was everything Headmaster wanted in a child, highly intellectual, with an ability to learn very quickly. By his teenage years Mumba was playing a number of musical instruments, and as well as speaking several of our languages, he spoke fluent English and French all while excelling in school. Headmaster expected all his children to be excellent, in a similar if not better way than Mumba. He felt this as a parent, a visionary and because of the pressure to convince his people, that what he had in mind would work. How his own children were perceived was important.

For every sibling following a golden child, pressure was the order of the day. The children at school took to bullying Headmaster's eldest daughter Makesa, she was less secure and invested in being regimented in comparison to her brother. The fact Headmaster had almost impossible expectations, meant she was a receptive recipient of abuse from the other stressed-out pupils at the school. Headmaster ran a very strict regime and for many children his methods felt unbearable at times. Children took to impersonating him in Makesa's presence and would often heckle him after he had given a school directive and was out of earshot. While Mumba in his excellence could not care less what the other children thought, his life was also less stressful because he was mostly adored. For Makesa her father being Headmaster meant she was expected not to complain about the treatment she received from other children. Grasping specific concepts required extra work along with repetition on her part, and at the end of every school day she would be exhausted, only to continue schoolwork at home. Makesa found this life exhausting and sometimes joyless. Mumba noticed how much harder it was for his sister to obtain results that he achieved easily and decided to be her light relief in life. He would play music on the piano to prompt her to sing along and when she failed to do so, he would insist she sing along because he knew she loved singing. He was the only one who would tell jokes in a house that was almost always serious. Later in life, when she reflected on her childhood, she would realise that he had been the light at a time when life felt like pressure from birth.

Along with the keeping her amused, Mumba also helped Makesa with her schoolwork and homework. He shared all the tricks he had come up with to get out of doing non-school work around the house or even at school, those were the best stories because watching him in action would be another reason to be in on a joke or to stand in awe of his ability to engage everyone he met.

Mumba took to making her giggle during Shikulu's extended prayer sessions. After prayers ended, which sometimes meant

Makesa would then endure long lectures from Shikulu along with scripture referencing the folly that was a person who laughed without sense of occasion. Those lectures took as long as Headmaster felt his point had been made to the listener, if he judged the attention was not to his liking, the lecture went on for a longer stretch.

At school Grace not only met all expectations she exceeded the headmaster's son. Added to her intellect, she walked with seriousness that made Shikulu proud, she cared about order in her work and her environment. There was not a single school day that went by that Shikulu did not refer to the good qualities that everyone could learn from Grace. The boys envied this attention and in general every 'praise for Grace' moment during assembly was met with rolled eyes. However, it had the desired effect because more children than not watched Grace and did their best to emulate her behaviour, her posture and worked to be as conscientious in all that they did just as Grace was.

Praise for Grace was not confined to school, everyone within the community and those in surrounding areas had heard about the amazing young lady at the new school. She was everybody's pride, and her name would often come up in conversation. Grace was better than a star, she was greater than hope, she was the future incarnate. In fact, she was Shikulu's word made flesh. He had predicted that a time was coming when the beauty of a woman, would be measured by her intellect and ability to shape the direction taken by the environment she inhabited. Grace never took sick days off school, she had no late days, as well as being orderly, Grace was a reliable pupil in the school. She was so dedicated that the first time ever she failed to attend class; it rang alarm bells in the teaching staff.

Mrs Lopi lived a simple life one that many today with their busy days would envy. She loved her job as educator, it was a role she found satisfying. She would have gone into teaching even if the invaders had not inserted themselves into their lives. As well as being a person of simple needs, she married a simple man. As a couple, they did not stand out, in that sense they were very well suited.

She was small in stature had deep brown eyes and if humility was a person, it would look like her. She loved her people and lived for the cultural rules of engagement in place. She was the aunty who would hear about an altercation within the community and counsel the person in error. When she intervened, it was always with the application of cultural and traditional practices, to help the parties involved reach peaceful resolutions. Mrs Lopi loved helping to resolve disagreements or misunderstandings. She was soft spoken and somehow always knew when it was the right time to speak, in moments of conflict.

Understanding the customs also involved knowing, what type of food to present when requesting that people hear you speak during an intervention. How the peace offering food was presented also mattered, uncooked generally meant the offence had been caused to an Elder, chicken was always a good place to start, the type of chicken mattered especially when requesting for an audience with an Elder and you wanted to be assured a warm welcome.

The greater the offence or crime, the larger the animal. However, it was unusual that a person making a peace offering was turned down, there was a general preference within the community to draw a line under a contentious matter and to move forward in peace. People asking for forgiveness, were never without other family representatives present. One or more members of the family always came along. Attending any important matters alone was not cultural practise, being lone entities was not a natural state for the community. The act of making amends also had to come from the family as a whole, which reinforced the understanding that our actions are never singular. Wounding one in a family meant their whole family had been affected. The transgression of one was and remains a collective transgression the same applied to success. Whilst apologies were never singular, the family of the one accused of causing offence, came along to show collective remorse. Others on the side that had been wronged were free to decline and denounce an act of contrition especially when the issue was perceived as standard error. Simple offences were considered problematic because everyone was supposed to learn and understand basic rules in place to avoid the occurrence of disharmony. Therefore, people were more likely to suspect an act was deliberate, if it fell under the heading of general misdeed. Standard transgressions also often raised the question of whether the family was doing the work involved in teaching those in their care about our culture.

Just as remorse was a collective act, accepting an apology was also a collective response and it was in this area that Mrs Lopi excelled, she had a very good understanding of what to do to reduce the likelihood of being sent away. Perhaps this skill was an inevitable result of all the time she had invested in connecting with individuals within their community. It could also be that everyone was right, and she lived partly on earth with her other part in the spirit world. They believed this gave her an advantage in how she approached the workings of the physical world. Her skill at resolving conflict also meant that she was immensely respected for using her gift to facilitate healing in others and not for personal gain.

Having Grace as a pupil in Mrs Lopi's class was for her like most other adults working with the young lady an honour. To be a part of nurturing what was a very special young lady was a gift in and of itself. Shikulu had emphasised the importance of maintaining the high standard they had set through the model student that was Grace. No adult in school dropped the ball where she was concerned. That is why on the second morning that Grace was not present in school, there was again concern though it remained unspoken.

Teachers at the school, were not prone to needless panic or overreaction. However, deep down Mrs Lopi feared that Grace's absence meant something serious could be amiss. She rationalised that perhaps Grace was simply unwell, and no one had thought to let them know. The problem was that she knew how driven Grace was, she suspected that Grace was the pupil who would attend school with a broken limb if needs be to achieve her goals. Mrs Lopi reminded herself that getting carried away with thoughts of what could be the wrong was not helpful. Besides Headmaster was not one to tolerate being dragged into matters not fully thought through. The dressing down she would receive would be severe. She decided to wait before speaking to him. Instead, she planned to put together concrete reasoning for raising alarm over Grace's lack of school attendance first. In a community where everything and everyone worked together, what could possibly happen to a child without someone knowing? No! She was sure everything was fine and would wait for Grace to return to school which would no doubt be anytime that week.

The following morning there was still no sign of Grace. Mrs Lopi wondered if her attachment to the child had made her needlessly fussy. She contemplated going to Grace's home to check in on her, but after only three days she feared it would appear overzealous to the child's parents. Bearing in mind most of the people in the village had been reluctant to enroll their daughters into the school to begin with. It would be unwise to appear to be making a nuisance of herself with the family. No! She had to wait a bit longer.

It was coming on to the end of the week, Mrs Lopi had tentatively enquired among the other children if they had seen or heard anything about Grace, but her enquires led to nothing that could explain the child's absence. The week ended with no news or explanation.

Grace's father was a fisherman, this meant work started early for them, her mother worked their fields during the day and Mrs Lopi wondered if she could pay a visit under the guise of being helpful, they might receive her visit better. Then she remembered how obnoxious Grace's father was and how much coaxing had gone into getting permission for not just one but two of their daughters to attend school. The other daughter would start when she was of age, Mrs Lopi wondered if it was worth risking irritating them. Headmaster had already caused enough people in the village annoyance with his know-it-all demeanor.

Everyone thought Headmaster walked with an air of superiority, he spoke many of the Indigenous languages and added French which he learned from Belgian nuns and English to the list. Not only that he declared for all to hear that he was a visionary. But the English were fast decimating Mitondo's way of life, Shikulu was believed to be one of their last chances of hope in retaining their identity. So, they tolerated him. It was useful that he knew to keep the imperialists happy with the thought that the natives were conforming, he did this long enough to blind them to the truth which was that everyone was preparing mentally at least to fight them off when the time was right.

Then she came up with a brilliant plan, she would visit the family for informal reasons. After all their culture was one of welcoming others, they would not question outright what her intentions for the visit were. She would take Cassava with her as a gift and sit with the women in the compound. Surely, she would be able to find out what was going on with Grace if she stayed with them long enough. On her day off she packed the Cassava in a Chitenge cloth and walked to Grace's family compound. She had brought enough to give the Elders their own and for others to share among themselves. She had enough ubupe (gift) to be appropriate. There were four houses in total on the compound and behind their houses was the vast land that the women and young people mainly farmed, while the men were fishing or hunting. It was the women who practiced rotation of

53

crops and for the most part this system worked well enough for them that nobody went hungry.

Champe known as Shi Mwape - father of Mwape – because in this culture parent's names changed to reflect the fact, that they were parents. Some interchanged their children's names, especially when a couple had more than one child. But most stuck with the name of the first born, even spouses referred to each other in those terms. Later when culture evolved and twins (ba mpundu) were understood not to be bad omens, every parent with twins whatever the order of birth within the family, was referred to as mother or father of twins.

Champe had been in charge of the compound since his father transitioned to the next life. As free movement had now been curbed by the invaders, the task of being head of the compound was less complex. Champe's father had ongoing stories that were shared of his leadership, and his success was a point of pride for his immediate and future descendants. People from distant villages knew of him and marrying into his family ensured security and good health especially for the offspring. There was also the prestige of being part of a strong family history.

Champe had inherited the success of his father who had advanced their family name, so much so that sometimes it felt like there were no new ideas left for Champe to capitalise on. He lived insecure that everyone in the village believed, his story would likely remain that of one who inherited and had not added to greatness. He feared his name would be remembered as a man who but for his father's greatness would be nothing. This kept him up many a night.

To compensate Champe woke up earlier than everyone, worked harder than all those he hired to work for him, he ensured that days of rest were enjoyed by all with Chibuku flowing freely. The Elder men had a special place allocated to them on his compound, where they could watch their families have fun as they enjoyed days off work. He worked hard to look after all the people in his care making sure that they were happy. Yet it was still not enough to fill the void in his heart.

He loved all his nieces and nephews; his people came to him or his mother to resolve matters among them and avoid issues escalating to the Chieftain. He was fair, had managed to maintain success, but he still felt like a small man. There was a level of respect his father received, that he believed he did not get. People tended to forget themselves around him, in a way they would never have done around his father when he was alive. Champe avoided reminding people their manners because he feared his insecurities would show. But he noted their lax attitude to tradition and conduct around a man of his stature and he quietly hated it. For all his hidden insecurities, what Shikulu would do to him one afternoon would be the final straw in the long line of disrespectful incidents, in which Champe had been forced to bite his tongue.

To Champe's dismay, Headmaster had walked into his compound without announcing himself as would be culturally correct. Normally sending a child to let the Elders of a compound know of a guest's intention to visit was the correct way. Instead, Headmaster simply arrived unannounced and went on to speak to the women about education for all girls. Champe watched him animated as he discussed his brilliant idea to include girls in his educational program. He watched Headmaster explain, how the current system of marrying girls off at a young age was not going to help them in the new world. Headmaster shared with the women how future women would be seen as beautiful for being intelligent, rather than presently where beauty was measured by a smile that revealed perfect teeth and could warm hearts or a full and shapely figure, which was soft enough for a man to rest his head. In this community features believed to be fertility indicators were highly sort after. But on a purely superficial level every man wanted a wife with a beautiful face.

On that day Headmaster's actions in Champe's eyes had dethroned him, and he was incensed. Falling back on old habits he decided to refuse to publicly acknowledge the disrespect. He would let the visit pass as though it was nothing, that would be his way of returning disrespect to Headmaster. In normal circumstances Champe would have complained to Headmaster's people and asked that they rectify this offence. But he decided to save face it was easier to treat Shikulu as though he was of no importance. Champe thought to himself as he watched his offensive guest "Let Shi Mumba talk to the women all day; we'll see where that gets him". He remained seated under the tree watching until Headmaster left, without so much as a look in the head of the compound's direction.

That evening Champe's mother came to his home, played with the grandchildren for a while, sat down for a meal with his wife, and just before she left, dropped the bombshell that she wanted all the girls of the compound to be allowed to attend school. He sat silent, knowing that his mother being an Elder had to be allowed to speak. He could have gone against her, but he had spent years trying to show that like his father he understood changing tides. Champe felt his hands were tied, he agreed with his mother, but he was angry. Had Headmaster come to him respectfully, he would have had no problem consenting to all the children attending school. Everyone in the village knew he was a reasonable man. Many had said as much to Champe when they spoke about how he was viewed by others in conversation. Why would a man he felt was his equal disrespect him in this way?

Shinganga - spiritual doctor - had been watching what had transpired. He concerned himself with making observations that he could put to good use at the appropriate time. At this point Shinganga had complex and pressing reasons behind his decision to invest time watching interactions within the village. Unlike the rest of the residents, he was fairly new, his roots were not from Mitondo. The rest of the people had long links with every family within the community. His presence among them came about because, he had managed to convince enough people that he had a link to the spirit world. A skill that everyone in the community was aware of, from time to time some among them had sought the help of people with that gift. There was an unspoken acceptance that living among us were rare people who were able to see and hear what many could not.

They were highly respected and often never needed to do anything to obtain food, shelter or clothing as a result of their position within the communities. The gift they possessed made them almost sacred to the people that sought their wisdom. To many they were ranked higher than most local healers, who obtained their discipline and skills through years of studying the medicinal elements of roots, herbs, and live animals. As with most other skills and specialties in Mitondo, the study of medicine using naturally available resources on the land was passed down from one generation to the next within families especially to those that showed an aptitude for the skill.

Shinganga had a problem, in recent years with the arrival of the English, coupled with the community's own medical people plus the new religions. His practice was in danger of becoming extinct. He was also concealing a truth about himself. While his people may have had some among them who could communicate with the spiritual world. That specific access to the spirit realm was not his gift, however he had expert understanding of human behavior. Shinganga was so successful at deceiving others that he possessed the gift, people rarely ever suspected he was a fraud. He often guessed correctly what could be wrong with those consulting him, especially as most cases were regarding common human problems. He then cloaked the guessing in a veil of mystery, and mostly this was enough for those that consulted him to believe he had supernatural powers.

Shinganga lived by a rule, to avoid making grand predictions, this was to reduce instances of his prophecies being questioned after failing to manifest. On the occasions someone returned having not had the promised results, Shinganaga would invite them into his home on a specified day. Being an expert at deception, he ensured every movement he made was shrouded in an air of mysticism. The process would often begin with him burning incense till his small room was saturated in a cloud of smoke and overpowering scent. He would then sit in silence with the client/s, making the odd body jerk and sound, and when enough time had passed, and he was convinced they were sufficiently immersed in his charade. He would slowly open eyes sing a short song with slight sobbing sound in his voice, a sound that can only be produced by African male singers. Then eventually speak slowly and deliberately explaining that the spirits protecting his client's foe were powerful. Depending on the level of acceptance he sensed from the client he would play up the danger involved and take the opportunity sell them another protection plan. On the odd occasions he thought about the things he had asked people to do to maintain his deception, Shinganga felt sure he would pay for it in the next life. Then he would remember that it was not for him to worry about the next life, while starving in this life and laughed to himself. He was very good at his job; he was just not magic.

Being a patient man, he had waited for the right opportunity to overthrow every new system squeezing him and real Shingangas out of business. Headmaster's arrogance gave him the opening he needed; the man was Baptist and the worst kind. The kind that points out all other people's inadequacies then rubbed their noses in the fact that by God's grace, he remained disciplined, educated, gifted and had never taken a single mind-altering substance. A clean life to a Puritan was equal to a clean mind and Spirit.

Shinganga had also heard the children talk about lessons they were being taught that he felt sure were of direct threat to him and others like him. Apparently, Headmaster had been teaching the children that talking to the spirit world was not possible, that men like Shinganga were lying about having supernatural powers. The children were being taught that the only powers possessed were the ability to poison people or feed their victims unsavory things, that would result in making them poorly or even die. The school was teaching children that everything Shingangas claimed to be supernatural could be explained, and there was nothing special about them. In doing so Headmaster was threatening Shinganga's only means of living. Fraudulent and criminal behavior was something the people were aware of. Children were cautioned either at school or by their elders of the dangers of eating in households not permitted. It was just as well that many of Shinganga's service users never found out what most of the potions he gave them contained. Many had stomach-churning ingredients that could induce sickness just thinking about. His potions included anything from pubic hair, nails, menstrual blood, dog faeces added in food and given to an unsuspecting person. He often included nauseating ingredients in many of his love potions. He preferred to mix in animal excrement with all other herbs. For anyone wishing to conceive a child of a specific gender, the process would involve making the husband eat food with drops of menstrual blood added in. As for keeping a partner faithful, there was the less unpleasant ingredient of sourcing breast milk to be added to his concoction. For all his customer's requests Shinganga would ensure to ask for the most outrageous ingredients from the person in need and in doing so tying them both to the act. This had the added benefit of users being less likely to speak out should the potion not work. The Shinganga profession even real ones were often spoken about negatively, it was well known that in every matter they intervened there would be tears in the end for someone. There appeared to be no way for them to apply their skills for good. Yet there were always people desperate enough or did not care, how the outcome backfired on them as long as they obtained their desired objective. It was primarily the need for revenge that kept their business thriving. His business had been ticking along very well until men like Headmaster started filling the people's head with unhelpful ideas about his profession.

Shinganga had already noticed a reduction in reverential fear, compared to what he had been accustomed to. If he was honest with himself, he would have acknowledged the truth that most people currently using his service were humouring him. Many were becoming aware of his lack of talent, from other people's bad experiences. Adding those that caught on to his ruse, to the numbers converting, as well as those influenced by the external education, it meant business for him had been lean for some years. People seeking his intervention was close to none. In fact, revenge and those reduced to turning to him in desperation after having tried all other ways, was now his main source of income. It had become insulting; he had gone from being one of the first point of call to an embarrassing last. As he had never bothered to learn another skill, this was a desperate time for him.

However, after he witnessed Shikulu's display he realised, western arrogance had finally rewarded his patience. He knew that if he handled the situation with Champe well, he could dispense with the educators and the Christians in one fell swoop.

Having an advanced understanding of human behaviour meant that, Shinganga knew Champe's secret. Even without speaking to him, he had noticed that the man walked like an imposter. But rather than undermine him as Shikulu had done. He made sure his every encounter with Champe was respectful and filled with gratitude. Shinganga went so far as to declare to the right ears that he blessed the day the head of their compound was born. Champe enjoyed his encounters with Shinganga, it secured his thinking that he had managed to fool everyone into believing he deserved his position. Those moments with the spiritual man allowed his mind some respite from the constant self-doubt. On those days of confidence Champe was prone to bouts of generosity and kindness.

Shinganga rolled up his best snuff and walked up to Champe, he greeted him using his formal name as everyone in the village did.

Shinganga (flicking imaginary flies from either side of his head with his swot) said: Ba Shi Mwape I hope you awoke well in this morning?

Champe replied I am just here enjoying my hard-earned day of rest.

Shinganga : I noticed you had a guest, had I known I might have brought out my special brew as a welcome gesture.

Champe's face changed as he answered: That was not planned, I was as surprised as you to see Headmaster on this compound, he failed to give or send greetings, nor did he show the proper respect to the Elders of the household.

Shinganga saw his chance to suggest a way that would allow Champe to express his displeasure much more distinctly. He planned to present his idea in a way that handed Champe his opportunity to see to it everyone extended him the respect that came with his senior position. All the while concealing Shinganga's desperate situation. Shinganga, decided it was prudent to allow the head of compound to think that he was merely imparting advice out of concern for propriety. The spiritual healer wanted him to believe that all he had in mind was the good of Champe's household.

Once the Chibuku had been brought over, Shinganga delicately and with all the humility he could muster, began his suggestion to Champe about how he could approach his current problem. Champe was a receptive audience, Shinganga started by tapping into Champe's concerns that the new ways were watering down valuable traditions. Ways which had kept them orderly and safe for as long as anyone could remember. He weaved into this discussion the disrespect he had witnessed from Headmaster, adding that the new ways were not about respect or the preservation of our lives. Courtesies that made our heritage so beautiful were now looked down upon and not just by the from another land people who did not know better either. It was worse coming from those that had grown up in the beauty of our song and were choosing to forget and allowing themselves to be seduced by new ideas. To witness some among us choose to discard our ways was causing a seismic shift in the foundations of our stability as people, even in our internal wars, our song never ceased.

"Everyone is aware that this new threat was different, Shinganaga continued. But if too many of us turn our backs on our ways, no one can imagine what will happen to us. What would our children have as a source of internal security and knowledge to pass on to their children? What would they give to the world having discarded the story of their own source of life, and the things that had sustained them up to that point?" After speaking in African proverbs and inhaling snuff they diverted onto lighter matters, so much so that it felt random when Shinganga raised the topic of his concern for the children in their community and how he foresaw that a time was coming when parents would have no say in their children's lives. Then with all the depth, he could conjure up he emphasised how worry for the children's future kept him up at night. Shinganga was not wrong, the new arrivals had been systematically erasing everything that represented them. They were ruthless and took advantage of our people's instinct to welcome and take in strangers. By now it was clear that getting rid of this new presence would take wars no one could fathom. However right Shinganga was, he was also wrong because the core of his intention was self-preservation, all that mattered to him was maintaining the aspects of his culture that kept him well-fed, revered and looked after. The reverence he received was nothing to sniff at either. What he found most upsetting was our people had managed to care for the very ravenous invaders who took without sowing back, yet when it came to him the care was slowly being withdrawn. He had become surplus to requirement, and the invaders were the gift he needed to claw back relevance.

Shinganaga advised Champe to begin by exercising his right as head of the compound, he humbly asked Champe to assert his authority immediately within his home, while there was still time to be the example the rest of the community needed. He suggested that removing the girls from school should be the first course of action after all who wants a girl who is western educated when their greatest currency was their childbearing ability? Despite wanting the girls to return to normal Mitondo duties, even Shinganaga accepted that the invaders were a problem, and added that there was no sense in removing the boys from school. At least that part of Headmaster's limited plan to felt like good sense. Both men agreed that the need to study the invaders was a pressing matter.

With every word he uttered he was handing Champe the cause he had been searching for whole his life. This anti-western education and aversion to the new religion was the foundation, he would build his legacy upon. Champe could finally set himself apart and show everyone that not only was he his father's son, but that they were safe in his capable hands.

The morning Mrs Lopi arrived at their compound, Champe walked with an air of authority, he had put together a strategy and over the days that followed Headmaster's misstep, the two men had worked through all the kinks. Now Champe was ready to execute the ideas that would establish him as the undeniable bedrock of security within his compound. He felt so good on the day their ploy had been finalized that he decided that evening he would invite his second wife to sit with him in the main home, then follow it up with an intimate encounter. This might even be the day he would make another child with her, the way he was feeling, the child produced would be given a name worthy of the definition of strength.

Champe had informed everyone on the compound not to deviate from his instructions, he told them not to improvise because he knew what was best and they were to follow his word to the letter. He ordered that his wishes remain respected in the event anyone from the school other than Headmaster came to visit. He emphasised that going against his wishes in any way was as good as directly going against him.

Having arrived at Champe's compound, Mrs Lopi was unaware that there was a problem and was therefore unguarded. She was welcomed by the women, and children were sent to inform the male Elders of her arrival. She proceeded to follow the traditional process of greeting, maintaining respect for all Elders, while presenting them with the gifts she had brought as way of thanking them, for welcoming her into their space. After this Mrs Lopi returned to sit with the women. Champe was impressed with her humility, her greeting made him wonder for a moment if things would have been different, had she been the one to ask their permission to educate the girls. Perhaps he might have felt less resentment. Champe knew that part of his father's skill was taking what was good from the groups of people they met along their travels. Then using the lessons enrich his own clan. His father also shared warnings of destructive behaviours he had witnessed, his aim being to always be better after learning even from those that were broken.

Mrs Lopi's appreciation of their ways warmed his heart. Educators within their village were arrogant, unlike educators of the cultural ways, who placed greater value on teaching and sharing information as an act executed with an open hand and given freely. Somehow working with the invaders had changed how information was shared, and knowledge had become weaponised. Whilst our educators were revered, they never felt the need to make others feel less than, it was understood that what they knew was valuable, so the respect came without coercion or breaking souls in the process.

The general consensus in the village was that the new educators were not good. They shamed those that struggled to understand and worse they sneered at our spiritual ways. Most in the community did not feel they were in a position to argue this matter without Chieftain intervention and insecurity had already begun to take a hold of them. Many were becoming fearful to ask when they did not know, to avoid being called ignorant or backward. They fought their natural urge to remind the Indigenous educators that the new arrivals had made them forget who they were.

Mrs Lopi was different, she was able to curve and bend successfully between different communities including among those of the new ways. That day she sat on ubutanda (traditional straw mat) with the other women, and gently asked after everyone. Respectfully she probed the women, in the hope of obtaining information of Grace's whereabouts. All her attempts to steer the conversation to Grace were expertly thwarted, at this point she had no idea that they were deliberately being evasive. The family had rallied around Champe, and his wishes were going to be respected. No one wanted to be the one to break his trust.

Mrs Lopi: Abana bali shani (How are the children)

High ranking wife (HRW): Awe bwino fye bonse (they are all ok)

Miss Lopi: Bushe abesa kusulu bonse bali temwako? (Do all those that attend our school enjoy it)

HRW: Ala bonse aba lumendo bali ku temwa elo nga bati bailange amano awe chakusseka:

(All the boys love school, you should see them showing off their intelligence. it's very funny)

Every time the HRW within the community spoke, her responses were confirmed with nods and smiles in all the right places by the other wives and women. It was then that Mrs Lopi became afraid. History and her own experiences had taught her that when our people became guarded in this way something bad had happened and she feared that Grace was in danger. Convention did not allow her push or intrude but every fiber of her being was compelling her to run all around the compound searching for the child. She knew that she could not take this matter to the Chieftain because if she was wrong, there would be no turning back from the damage caused and reparations would have to be made for overstepping and offence caused.

Mrs Lopi was taken back to a time as a young person when she had gone with her cousin to the river. It was the day they washed their clothes and out of nowhere they saw a man from their community walking up to them. Everyone knew that there were segregated spaces for children and those for adults. The way he looked at them was alarming. They tried to ignore him, but he kept talking to them as though he had not broken an important rule. All adults knew not to go where the young girls bathed or washed their clothes, the same went for the place young boys bathed. The girls suspected this man's intentions were not good and they hoped he would go away, but he kept talking and walking towards them.

The look on his face continued to cause them discomfort, without words they looked at each other and ran. They ran on the stony pathway screaming as they did, to alert others, but also in the hope it would frighten him. However, on this day his deep urges for the children had taken over his mind. He ran after them undeterred. Mrs Lopi's cousin fell back and before long he had caught up with her. He raped her, then when his madness had been satisfied. He attempted to conceal what he had done by further breaking other parts of her body, to make her death appear to have been the result of falling, while running unreasonably from him. He planned to insist he meant the children no harm.

Despite all attempts by healers who worked to save the young girl, the injuries were too severe, and mercy finally found her on the night she transitioned in her sleep.

The man changed his story a number of times. He first claimed to have ended up in that area by accident and meant them no harm. He insisted the injured child had fallen badly after overreacting to seeing him, and that was what caused her death. Finally, after questions over the injuries to her private area were asked, he changed his story this time accusing the young girls of seducing him first and in a moment of madness he went along with it. His inability to maintain the same story and young Mrs Lopi's constant account led to everyone in the compound agreeing that this matter was serious enough to refer to the Chieftain. By the time their compound had agreed to escalate the matter, the child rapist and murderer had run away. His wife and children remained, and his shame was theirs especially his children. Deviance was perceived as a trait that ran in the blood, no one would start a family with them. It would have been easier to leave but his wife decided that they would remain and all that was left of his DNA in his five children would die out in the village rather than spread his sickness to other parts of the continent. This sacrifice meant she was respected but everyone knew not to marry or reproduce with his children.

Mrs Lopi always believed that had they acted sooner, perhaps her cousin's murderer might not have gotten away. But tradition, the steps, the order they were required to follow could be frustratingly long at times. She was determined that Grace would end up another tragic unresolved story.

Grace was intelligent, she was not beautiful in a conventional way; she was what some might call plain. The sort of child whose father might interrogate a suitor extensively because if he was not motivated by physical appearance why was he there? Fathers were not willing to send their children into a life of abuse even if they were girls. Grace had something special she was genius, everyone saw that even those outside the greater compound, she understood complex concepts from a young age and constantly exceeded expectations set for her. She helped design ways to improve life among them that made the community's day to day living easier.

However, despite Grace's obvious intelligence her family were more focused on when and whom she would eventually marry and start a family with. The only person who saw her as being greater than the roles of wife and mother, as noble as they were to others, was Headmaster. He wondered what good there was in procreating on perilous terrain. Grace loved how the headmaster and the teachers marvelled at her abilities. The day Headmaster called her into his office and told her that she played a main role in his vision to educate young girls. She went home walking on air, humility meant she could not share this wonderful news with her family, but that day gave her life meaning, she never knew she needed.

Grace was taught the sciences, history, ours and theirs, geography, mathematics and other languages including those in our country she did not know. She excelled in all subjects but one, languages, specifically those foreign to the continent were difficult for her to grasp. She saw the disappointment on Shikulu's face at this short coming, language was key, and she understood that. Though she struggled with that aspect of learning Grace spent days and nights practicing languages she had been assigned; she was determined to be better than any of the other children in every way.

Back at Champe's compound, the verbal dance Mrs Lopi was locked in, was coming to an end she had failed to illicit out of the women what was going on with Grace. By now she knew that they were choosing not to tell her. It was not her place to push the matter, but she had to tell Headmaster what was going on.

The next school day, Mrs Lopi went to see Shikulu, she was nervous but knew leaving it any longer would make her the target of his outrage. Meekly she entered his office. Shikulu was not friendly, he was never welcoming, she was aware that having stepped in the room, he was already feeling impatient at how long she would take before returning to work. When she informed him, that Grace was not in school and for how long she been absent, he looked more thoughtful than angry or concerned. He asked her to go back to work as he would speak with Grace's family. Mrs Lopi was confused but felt relief that she had at least conveyed her concern to someone who might be able to get to the root of the problem.

Culture Matters

Shikulu felt anger but at himself, he had invested too much in one person and now he was forced to engage families that should know by now how important this process was. All to find answers to a simply question such as where their child that was meant to be in school was? By the end of the day, he had decided this was a good lesson, he would begin the process of remedying this dependence on the hope that was Grace. Other talented children would be selected and trained; all the teachers would just have to work harder to advance the chosen few up to the high standard he had set. He was not ready to give up on Grace, and he planned to visit the family, with the aim of ending talks by emphasising the importance of consistency and following through with commitments. After all this was for everyone's benefit.

When he arrived home, he found a house full of people who were regularly fed by Lupapa. He felt proud of the family he had, at this point they had six children. His amazing wife somehow managed to make their home a wonderful place to live, and she had no one helping her, which was unusual for their community. Shikulu did not want to mix his home life with the people, to avoid familiarity as he needed to maintain his authoritative image. Aside from eating together, all his expectations for what his family should look like had been met by Lupapa and she was doing brilliantly, she even found time to continue being a mid-wife and medicine person. Shikulu was very proud of his wife.

 The truth was this deviance from the support system was drowning Lupapa, who refused to admit she was exhausted and at the end of her tether. Shikulu may have been happy, but the children were not, and his wife was an impatient and mechanical mother rather than warm and kind like the other mothers. He was blind to this reality. In his mind his family life was perfect

That evening he wondered if it would be a good idea to invite Champe and his people to eat, he felt sure that with Lupapa's charm he would come to a happy understanding with them. Shikulu had noticed that the men of Shi Mwape's compound were not very receptive to him, a meal might be an opportunity for him reach out to the men of the family. Despite his guarded exterior, he wanted to be at peace with those around him.

The next day should have been like any other day in Lupapa's home. But on this day change needed to come, her silence was not honouring her life or her ancestors. She was stretched beyond belief, she realised she hated her life and did not know how to change things. She had done everything she had been asked to do by her husband, to the point of bleeding support for those who needed it. She had continued with healing and filling others with love just as she had done before marriage. By the time that love reached her six children it was deficient. Living this way had finally become too much, even for a formidable adaptable woman like her. When she arrived home that day, she was exhausted from working, cleaning, & cooking among other things. She called out to her daughter Makesa, the child was late in executing her chores this was not the first time she had done that. She lacked discipline and was only concerned with having fun. On this day Lupapa had had enough, after calling out her name a second time she was done with having to repeat herself. "Did not these children realise how much work she had, on any given day? Or maybe they did not care? Did anybody care?" She left her home with rage seeping from all the places that her new life had betrayal of her, as she hunted for Makesa. She could not see clearly for the rage, she finally looked up, and there at the very top of a Guava tree laughing and happy was her daughter. This infuriated Lupapa. The disrespect, and not being seen coupled with the rage in her, at watching her child play while she was stretched beyond belief. Lupapa did not remember climbing the tree or slapping Makesa so hard that she fell out of the tree and broke all her front teeth.

By the time she had climbed down and saw the extent of the child's bleeding, her rage had dissipated, all that was left was her deep remorse and a bleeding child with a very swollen face. She tried her best to comfort Makesa but the damage was done and could not be hidden or fixed with hugging, begging or medicine. Lupapa begged Makesa for forgiveness, not only because of the shame she felt but also because she knew Shikulu was against physical punishment of the children. That day Lupapa made excuses to their regular dinner guests, she knew that when Headmaster came home, she needed the family alone for what would come. When he arrived and saw Makesa's her face swollen to the point of being unrecognisable, as Lupapa tried frantically to explain how sorry she was and how she never meant to hurt their child, adding that and had she been in her right mind... before she could finish her words, Shikulu looked at her and said. "I left a healthy child, and I will not return home until she looks as I left her this morning", with that he walked out of their home.

Lupapa took herself to the Chieftain, feeling like failure, broken and knowing she had wronged everyone, she explained what happened. When they saw the child, even with remedies the injuries were extreme. Makesa was called to speak with the Chieftain without her father or mother present. They asked Makesa if this was how the children lived with Tata and Mama beating them? She told the truth, that Lupapa never tended to their emotional needs like the other mothers, that she was angry more times than not and busy all the time. Makesa told how unlike the other children, they were separated from everyone which meant playing and moments of childlike joy were rare. She told them how Shikulu made them all stay up till the early hours working sums or some other school practice on a board.

Shikulu was called first to answer for the things they had heard were happening in his home. He insisted Lupapa was to blame, they ordered him to allow young people to help Lupapa around the home since he objected to having grownups in his home. They told him his wife would need to re-enter the women's community on days of rest and festivity. They insisted he do that, if he planned to avoid disaster falling upon all the people by what would happen next in his home. Shikulu knew that refusing was not an option unless he wanted to leave the entire community.

Lupapa was summoned next, she was chastised for going against the way our mothers lived and going against everything she knew to do and finally because a child was nearly lost, they had to be reparations. Makesa was called into the room only after, they had finished letting Lupapa know what they had decided to avoid a repeat of what had transpired. They reiterated her action had endangered the whole community. When Makesa joined them, the Chieftain asked her, to think of a worldly element, she wanted her mother to give her as repayment for the crime committed against her. She asked for a bicycle. Lupapa was told she would have to find the means not by her husband or her people to provide the bicycle for the child. They added that now she would have the support she had rejected, her main priority until their next meeting was to serve her daughter.

Shikulu was angry at having to humble himself in front of the Chieftain. Lupapa's failure was also his and it could not have happened at the worst time. He decided inviting Champe to his home was no longer an option. By now word will have gone round and whilst the principle was for the community not to hold judgement after Chieftain interventions, the fact that his home needed healing in that period, meant no one would see him or his wife as a viable place for counsel or sanctuary for a while. He never told her, but he resented what he felt was her weakness, being a good believer, he was sure, he would soon release her from his anger but for now, he could hardly bring himself to look at her. He convinced himself that inviting Champe to his home was never a good idea anyway. Order, structure and good leadership was what the people needed to see. They already feared him, his stature helped maintain the mythology of him being all knowing and almost all seeing. He planned to use all the aspects of him, body and reputation to intimidate and compel Champe to let him know what had happened with Grace and end with how he expected future communication concerning the children to be conducted.

Once again on a day of relaxation Headmaster went to Champe's compound only this time, they were ready for him.

From the moment he arrived he was made to wait, this was jarring because it went against all their rules of welcome, by now Shikulu knew something was not right, but he failed to adjust his plan of engagement. Champe asked some children to invite all the other men from their homes, as he required them to sit in on the meeting under the tree. Only until everyone was seated, and a massive Chibuku clay pot placed in the middle, to be passed around as the men spoke, did Champe invited Headmaster to join them and speak. This time Shikulu realised it was time to adjust his approach and listen, everything he had witnessed upon his arrival bore the hallmarks of a very serious meeting.

He approached calmly and respectfully; he expressed his hope that they had all woken well on that day. They all confirmed this to be case but the heaviness in the air remained. Shikulu decided to get to the point. He looked at Champe and began by sharing with him how amazing Grace was, he showered praise on the child and those listening nodded along, but still the energy levels were low, until finally Shikulu got the point of why he had made his visit. He turned to Champe and began his lengthy attempt to find out why Grace had not been in school for some time. The school had not heard anything to explain her absence and for such a conscientious pupil it felt out of character, with any other child he could understand but Grace was different. Shikulu then asked if she was unwell?

Champe cleared his throat and knowing how much Shikulu detested alcohol he helped himself to another long gulp of the drink, all his actions were done in a deliberately slow and painful manner. Champe then leaned back into his stool and after what felt like a very long thoughtful pause he said:

Champe: Shi Mumba, was it not you, who came to this compound and disregarded me and our ways? In fact, you thought so little of me, you chose to speak only to the women.

Shikulu said nothing and continued to listen.

Champe continued: Shi Mumba do you recognise my position here?

Shikulu replied: I came to speak with the women because I thought that would be the best place for me to start explaining the importance of girls joining the school.

Champe: After my father's death, do you know who was left to care for the compound.

Shikulu was irritated at this point but tried to maintain civility. However, he refused to be made to answer basic questions as though he were a child. Instead, he said nothing.

One of the men interjected: Shi Mumba was raised by outsiders perhaps in his case it is as the saying goes, how can we expect a child to have wisdom where the mother did not?

All the men nodded, this was an obvious insult to Headmaster, and he saw it as such, against his better judgement and control, anger at this disrespect overcame him. He looked at the man and asked, "would you find it acceptable for any man in this community to speak to another in this way?"

The man responded, "All the men of this village were in taught our ways; I would never say this to them because they would never behave in the way you do".

Headmaster by now completely consumed with rage and responded "I have not come here to insulted by ba shita mbwa (men who buys dogs for a living), men who drink and make fools of themselves in the village. Nine Mwata (I am a Chief) you have all forgotten yourselves. I have returned to educate you, because I want to add to us, and this is how you speak to me. Nine Mwata ba fimbanamililo, mwaikalila ukunuka isabi nganu tamuli kunchito (I am a Chief, and you remain people who still only use fire to keep warm, men who smell of fish all day despite not being at work).

The men sat in silence as his voice roared. When he had finished with his tirade, Champe spoke.

"You may be a Chief, but this is my home, you have no say here unless it's your plan to change that. Please let us know if this is yet another adjustment you wish to impose on us. Then let us see what the people will say. You have dishonoured me in my own home and rather than leave to return with offerings and an apology you insult us. How many of our people have we fed and continue to feed, with the fish smell that you saw fit to insult us about? How many times have you, been sent the finest fish from me with no expectation, but simply a desire to honour you and what you do for us?"

Headmaster stood in silence, the men present sat in still and it dawned on Headmaster that this was not a matter he could fix, even with his pride he knew he had wronged Champe. He sat back down only to stand again and say "Ba Shi Mwape you have a gifted child, a real blessing to you and your people. I will speak to my people, and we can return at a later date to give offering and ask forgiveness as you have rightly suggested. But do not allow what was not meant as offence, to affect your talented child and how she moves forward from this point on. I promise you when she is finished with this education system, she will be known in every home, she will be our people's pride and joy, give me time and I will see to that."

Champe responded with a smile on his face "How do you suggest a married girl might balance going to school, maintaining this vision of yours, and running a home while taking care of the children that are to come"?

Headmaster was confused and responded that the child would need to finish this aspect of school, then the next, after which she could marry. Champe clarified, "Grace is now a married girl, we found a good family that was happy to have her as a daughter, they know of her intelligence and her ideas that have made life easier here. To them we were giving them a gift far greater than anything they had to offer. They are a very good family and importantly passionate about our ways". He explained how he did not hesitate to marry Grace off to them. All matters had been settled, dowry paid, and she now lived in her new mother's home to be trained in their ways until she came of age to move into her marital home.

As he spoke, Headmaster described to his family later, how in that moment his legs turned to water and he could not stand, he sat down in shock. He asked Champe why he would do such a thing because of his transgression? Champe stood up and explained that Headmaster's transgression was what he needed to understand that the new ways were corrupt. They caused brothers to fight, they brought unrest and after watching for long enough he had decided there was nothing of their knowledge he wanted us to keep, except to warn others that the ways of the new arrivals were a poison. Then he sat down knowing full well his point had been made and an arrogant man had been put in his place. The men continued to drink while Headmaster sat waiting for the life to return to his legs and then he could leave. To him this felt like a death, and he mourned as though a death had occurred.

But Ba Champe was not finished. After the talk, he instructed the women to speak to all their sisters within the compound and then the wider community, he was smart enough to know that a total boycott of the school would require further discussion and general consensus. He asked the women to instead encourage every mother and daughter that school was a good thing to attend until marital age which was 13 at that time. The idea was for the girls to go to school, if they wished with the understanding that it was not something for them to fully apply themselves. The plan was to sell it as a distraction until they were ready to marry. The mothers were surprisingly receptive, many were concerned at having their daughters wait too long before marriage. This conflicted with their understanding of prime conception age. Once they had been empowered with the knowledge that it was their choice, mothers whose children were of age pulled their daughters out of school immediately. When Shikulu was told what was happening to the girls in the school, he looked at his wife that night and said, "Our people are fools we need the girls and women". On that day he decided it would be easier to begin by galvanising his family around his vision. He knew this way would take longer, but that was how it needed to be done for now.

While Champe kept himself busy empowering the people by making Headmaster small in their minds. Shinganga focused on explaining to everyone in the community exactly what happens when we turn away from our ways. Many were so relieved to have clawed some power back from what felt to them like Shikulu's tight grip on their families. They were happy to entertain, a Shinganaga who had never given an accurate prediction in the whole time they had known him.

For months Lupapa watched Shikulu's broken heart make him lose taste for food, or all the other things he enjoyed, and she allowed it. The spirits had told her in her sleep that when the time to speak to him was right, then she could share what they had instructed her to say to him. She watched the people see him broken, but to her he was softening slowly, she would wait until he was internally receptive enough for her words to reach his soul. Then she would seal him up for his protection and his mind to carry on.

The night before he was ready the ancestors came to her in a dream and showed Lupapa what she needed to do next. Ancestors do not speak and instruct as such, when you meet them in your dreams, the message on what to do next only becomes clear when the person awakes. At the point of seeing them in a dream, ancestors only give what is physically needed to complete a task. If it's the strength to be able to stand that is what is directly told in the dream, if it is the discipline to be still then, that is what will manifest after an encounter in the dream. The understanding that followed such a dream could be as simple as, realising that a person around you is not being truthful and how, their face and the reason remains on your heart when it's morning, the same goes for all messages given to be passed on to others. Matters not involving the dreamer or those close to them are rarely issues ancestors touched upon with a third party, unless it is absolutely necessary.

That night when the ancestors called Lupapa they sat with her and shared our history with her, as they spoke, she felt perfect peace, which she needed having had a series of difficult months. They told her the stories that would give her wisdom for what would follow, then they made her lie still in calm waters for her to be renewed. After what felt like a very long time, she awoke at the usual time to begin breakfast and bath water preparations for her family which at this point included nine children. That morning was the most peaceful she had felt in a very long time.

Shikulu woke up at his usual time which was 4 am, everyone was trained to wake up then, because before anything else could be done they had prayers which normally took an hour. Lupapa was walking with such peace around her, after observing this Shikulu thought for a moment how nice it would be to stay at home that day and be with his wife. But he was disciplined, and he went to work after eating. When he returned Lupapa had ensured the children had eaten and instructed to go to bed as soon as chores were complete. That night Shikulu ate alone, he did not notice very much, the sadness that had overcome him had also blinded him.

Mama prepared a stool for him to sit on with a massive basin filled with hot water and a delicious earth aroma floating from the water into the air. Then she invited him to come over for a massage. By then it was dark, and they had only a lamp in the room. Lupapa began by washing his head and immediately the scent of mild menthol opened his chest and aroused his other senses. This was the first time he noticed that the room is filled with steam. She spent a long time massaging his head before slowly moving on to his face, this time there was no scent that he could detect and he wondered if Lupapa had changed the water, but he did not ask her, he did not want to disrupt what she was doing. Shikulu also did not notice that tears were rolling down his face, all he knew was that with each stroke of his head, and as her hands eventually moved onto every part of his body, with each touch the weight he had been carrying was lifting. The weight of responsibility, the burden of being strong, the fear of trusting anyone with his plans and finally the pain of being alone. All the burdens his spirit carried in this world were falling off him. It was like her hands had taken a form of healing that he could not describe. He wondered why they had never done this before, then knew that he would never have allowed himself to rest and trust in this way. Lupapa loved and massaged his body for over an hour and when she was finished, he was exhausted and ready to go to bed but most of all he felt grateful. That was not the night for her to speak to him and she did not.

When his work week was complete, Lupapa sat with him as he rested, and said "Tata, let's reintegrate. Your plan, your vision, they are yours and you are free to share what you believe is best according to the level people are at. But we can only do that from within. Let us sing with our people, dance with them, let's talk to them for the sake of talking and when they cry from loss, let us mourn with them as well. But you and I must begin by re-joining the community and I'm sure when they see us willing to rejoin and honour them, they will become more open to hearing you, your timing must allow for the peace that reintegration will bring. Our whole family needs to rest and, sit with the grandmothers as they share stories of caution, love and laughter. Its hunting season maybe you can join the men when they go. What good is having a rifle that lives unused in our home?" Shikulu seeing his wife as if seeing her for the first time, he felt such relief that she was there with him during his difficult time. He realised that having exhausted his ideas it was time to listen to the only person that had stuck with him through it all. It occurred to him that he had not afforded her the same support and he felt some shame. After she had spoken and he reflected, as well as agreeing to start over as Lupapa suggested. He decided that he had interfered too much in the way his wife lived, and he wanted to correct that. He asked her forgiveness for having forced a lifestyle that caused her body and spirit harm. He told her that he no longer wanted their home to be a place that harboured fears of over familiarity, and if she needed other women to come and help her with her health or just to talk about things that women needed to discuss then he hoped she would she feel free to reach out for that support.

After agreeing on what to do next they moved forward with their new outlook.

It was an unremarkable day, when Kalwe their fourth child became unwell, they were sure it was nothing that rest, and her favourite meals could not fix. She had been struggling to move and for an active child it was unusual, her brother Kunda who was the closest to her, checked in on her, and nothing felt out of the ordinary. Makesa and Mumba being first and second were the best of friends in the family, it was only natural that Kunda and Kalwe would create a bond. The first two were bound by responsibility, discipline and hard work in everything they did. They were the face of Shikulu and Mama, so they were expected to behave as leaders and be responsible at all times. Kunda and Kalwe had none of the pressure and they took every opportunity to play and enjoy life. They behaved and did what they wanted in school and at home. They were allowed to take risks the first two siblings were not, and at a young age they were even allowed to learn how to use Shikulu's rifles and all his weaponry. For them life was for exploring. Shikulu had relaxed his approach after the first two. As a result, to the older siblings it felt as though Kunda and Kalwe were allowed to be out of control and expand the boundaries of their curiosity. This leniency was also actively encouraged by all the Elders. Kunda and Kalwe were known for mischief, they joined Elders during talks while others focused on duties that young people were expected to be getting on with. In fact, the whole community had become an open space for them to do as they desired. When everyone saw them, they would smile, and it was not unknown for the two to be fed by aunties who delighted in their playfulness. Mumba and Makesa found them irritating especially as manual labour never seemed to phase the two explorers. They would be given tasks or chores and somehow managed got them done with plenty of time to carry on with their pleasures. Physically strong and hardworking children were recognised and praised at Mitondo. Between Mumba and Makesa the two struggled to muster the strength and energy to get physical work done swiftly as well as their younger siblings could. The first and second took to rolling their eyes at their brother and sister's high energy and eagerness to please. They exchanged mocking looks when Kunda and Kalwe received praise for getting chores done quickly and secretly joked that one day one of them would break. That joke kept Mumba and Makesa amused to no end. But really, their banter regarding their younger siblings came out of envy for the two who had the freedom to do whatever they wanted.

On the day Kalwe fell noticeably ill, Kunda was by her side for much of the time. Later as Lupapa was washing her, Kalwe looked at her and said, "I feel really unwell". Knowing her child would prefer to fight through than admit to being poorly this concerned her. They had a saying that when death was coming to visit it brought along with-it confusion. Lupapa had her people coming over and her house was unusually busy, another of the children was also poorly, she knew Kunda could take Kalwe to the hospital in Congo without issue and she felt sure, they would both be back in the evening with medication to alleviate her daughter's symptoms. Kalwe was carried to the river by members of the family, when they arrived Kunda took her from his uncle and put her on the canoe, that was when his eyes opened, and he saw for the first time just how unwell she was. At some point as he was rowing, she looked at him and told him that she was tired but thought they should pray first. They said the Our Father, and she fell asleep. When the boat arrived at the Congo shores, he picked her up as she was still fast asleep and carried her to the hospital. The nurse did not tell him straight away that his sister's body may have arrived, but she was already gone. His best friend had left a while ago, without fanfare, just silence, at the age of 12. They said it was smallpox. He did not remember going back to tell his mother that she was gone, he did not remember what was said or Lupupa's reply, he did not even hear the crying.

At the funeral Spirit through a local healer walked up to everyone crying and explained to them that these two names

83

were caught in cycle of love and tragedy. There was no way to stop the cycle and refusing to use their names ever again was not an option. They would have to name the two everywhere in every home, to ensure the cycle got watered down, that was the only way to cheat death with the two names. She suggested to name one and not the other in households, the instinct to protect each other was strong between them, whether they came back as child to the other, sibling or partner, the impulse to save each other would always arise and they would be bound in a fight for life and death. Ideally name one not both in a home, skip generations and hopefully they can live lives without the inevitable tragedy.

Whilst this was helpful it was also hard to execute, every time there was a child about to join the world of the living, they chose and told the family their name. There had to be agreement among Elder members when a name was first suggested after having received the message through dreams or instances unique to that particular name. Following their culture and their belief to the letter meant, they had limited power over when Kalwe and Kunda chose to come back, in which gender or even in what home.

Meanwhile at the school as most of the girls had not returned, their numbers in school were depressingly low, much lower than Shikulu would have liked. But he had resigned himself to preparing his immediate family first. If he could get enough leaders out of his home and those in his school still willing, they could go on to educate others more receptive, he hoped that this could be another way to increase the numbers of people mentally capable of joining the struggle to extract the invaders. This was a slower route, but better than giving up altogether. He focused much of his teaching on the invader's operational strategies. Emphasising the importance of learning what invaders did when they arrived in new places, what they take and how, finally what tactics they employed to break others. The truth is by the time he was preparing the young minds, the country had gone past the point where being able to separate from them without losing something could be prevented.

Mumba as expected, completed secondary school without issue and Shikulu called him aside to discuss his future. Having assessed his grades and abilities Headmaster had confidence that Mumba was more than good enough to be put forward for a scholarship to study law at Oxford University in the UK. Shikulu was sure that Mumba was secure enough as a person and unlikely to be devoured by the unfamiliar terrain his father planned to send to him study and live. As soon as Mumba received confirmation of his final grades, which were in keeping with expectations. His scholarship followed shortly after.

Makesa was on course to complete secondary school the following year. She was told by her father that the road would be easier for her if she took up nursing. She did not like blood or bodily fluids, and it sounded like a lot of manual labour. Makesa would have preferred something in an office or law like her brother, but she dare not say what she really felt out loud. Children then did not argue with decisions made by parents over their lives. Makesa also accepted that at that point in time, as a woman it was the right decision.

Kunda was free to choose what direction to take, after secondary school and he aligned himself with freedom fighters through his local union.

The rest were still too young and besides that, were not burdened with the same expectations.

When it came time to leave for England, Mumba was called into an early morning meeting with Elders where he would be given blessings and have prayers for his safe journey. As long journeys were made in groups, when one went out alone, they were sent off with spiritual shields to protect them. The meeting was held very early before life begun stirring, it was believed the spirit world was much more accessible to people then. His father reiterated the importance of Mumba's trip, they discussed avoiding distractions as there would be plenty of time to indulge in worldly needs after his degree was complete. Others blessed Mumba with words of wisdom, he sat and listened until all the Elders had given him something of them, to take with him. They need not have worried; Mumba was made to walk in new lands with confidence and an air of belonging. He knew he would do well; he also knew that deviating from the plan was not an option, the pride he felt at being part of a solution for our people was greater than any physical enticements the world could present to him.

Upon his return Mumba, like his father recounted his experiences abroad in mechanical terms. He shared the routine he had adopted while there to ensure success, he discussed how well he did in comparison to other young people at the university. There was no talk of fear, doubt, discrimination, lust or friendship. Mumba had the foresight to make business connections with a high-profile law firm that also operated in their country, how he achieved such a feat was also shared with the community. He had made such a good impression and forged relationships with senior people the law firm during his work experience abroad, that they not only verbally promised him a job when he returned to his home. But they were true to their word and the role he had been promised was waiting for him on his return.

The only person Mumba shared the details of his journey fully was Makesa. Despite his effort to conceal what he considered unnecessary details of his trip; many were quietly aware that he had not given the full picture of his time away from home. Mumba immediately started working for the law firm and because he was a star on earth, his excellence was remembered by them even after his death decades later.

Mumba soon met the woman who would become his wife in the city, she was also from the same region as he was but different village. His wife was timid and very loving, like everyone in Mumba's stratosphere, she came alive by sheer virtue of being around him. They went back to Mitondo to marry, they held a was traditional wedding first, followed by a civil wedding. Everyone liked her for him. They felt she would support and add to him rather than hinder his ascent in life and when the couple returned home, she did just that. Mumba was growing into his role at work very well, and before long they had two sons whom his wife graciously allowed to be named after her husband's people. Mumba was the name of the first and Kunda for the second, soon enough she was pregnant with a third, this time it was a girl. Mumba was over the moon, his family life looked just as he had envisaged for himself. When Makesa watched Mumba's family she struggled to imagine a life more perfect than his.

As advised with her father Makesa had begun training as a nurse and her general determination to do well induced irritation in her peers. In no time she was being teased for being too keen and wanting to achieve firsts in all her academic grades, as a result she did not make many friends, however experience and her age meant that she was less concerned with making friendships. They were not part of her plans, and their approval of her was irrelevant. While Mumba had several friends and admirers as he aimed high, the opposite was true for Makesa, whose obvious ambition was despised by both men and women. She took comfort in the knowledge that the vision she was a part off was greater than any doubters. Her friends went out dancing and having young fun during their time at university. Young women and men naturally sought each other's company, and a few young women dropped out because they fell pregnant. However, Makesa merely observed these interactions always keeping her eye on the goal. The teachers were unforgiving and sometimes cruel, but she completed with high grades as was expected of her. Whenever any of Shikulu's children were away from home they were required to write letters keeping him informed of their status, Makesa did so until she completed her nursing course.

Kunda joined the union masquerading as a freedom fighting entity, he managed to get a job as supervisor of the men working in the mines, his role there was as strategic as it was a human rights endeavour.

He would recruit people fighting for freedom but also remained hidden in plain sight as he was not considered a concern or threat in terms of being part of an uprising. In comparison to most industries, miners were well paid because of the health risks that came with their job. The new arrivals felt the financial compensation for the high mortality risk was enough to keep the men happy and at the very least the family members invariably left behind were for the most part able to live a reasonable life. Kunda mobilised the men to renegotiate their work terms, the men had always known that price for the lives lost was too low in comparison to the gain made by the colonising entity. Kunda was not afraid of hard work, he was a tough person, and determined that the Black men's humanity be recognised. As a result, the men found it easy to trust him.

Kunda gave free financial education to families of all the miners, he did that because they had witnessed a large number of deceased miner's families fall into poverty as soon after their death.

He insisted upon this education even for those that struggled to fully understand financial management. He taught them the importance of buying land or a property, in fact as union representative he fought for all miners to have homes built that would be kept as part of the compensation package to their families for their loss. The invaders did not even argue, such was the value of the mines and a miner's role. The truth was the miners were asking for very little, Western men and their families were being set for generations courtesy, of the work these Black men were giving their lives for. A free modest home was a compensation in comparison?

Shikulu was unwell, he felt it but had not shared his concerns with anyone. Lupapa had only just delivered their eleventh child and he felt it was not the right time to raise his health condition with her. By then was well into his sixties and believed that illness could be expected. When both Mumba and Makesa had completed their higher education, he was over the moon. They began to plan a celebration, but a lot of things had changed in Mitondo, with many moving into cities and only a few people were left behind, in many ways life was much more sedate, and how they lived had transformed. No one remaining was particularly alarmed by the changes, they lived in acceptance that life changed all the time. When the celebration was finally confirmed everyone began looking forward to the chance for a happy distraction. The fact Shikulu's two children were returning home was reason enough to rejoice. Shikulu planned to sit them down and entrench the need to follow through with the constant work of reaching and freeing the minds of our people. Everyone in Mitondo came together to plan the welcome home festivities, they all had so much to ask the two that were returning, after having started work in the city, there was also excitement finally seeing Mumba's new young family.

Livestock would be slaughtered and eaten on the day selected, the immediate family of the two wanted for nothing. Everyone was bringing something to the celebration, because Shikulu and Mama's joy was all their joy.

One evening when everyone had retired for sleep, the river did something it had never done before or would ever do again. The tide began to rise and not stop, the water then began moving very quickly on land and continued to do so till somehow to everyone's shock the river swamped Shikulu's house and only his house. This was all the more surprising, because the house was located far away from the river's shore. The first the family knew of the powerful force of nature heading their way was when they were awoken by a loud noise and ran outside. Only to be covered in water. Fortunately, every member of Shikulu's household remained unharmed as they could all swim, the shock of being immersed in water did not overwhelm to the point of causing permanent physical damaged to any of them.

However, all their belongings and along with the memories they stored with were either swept away or destroyed. When the shock had settled, they noticed that only their home had been targeted by the river, all nearby houses remained untouched by water. Everyone knew this was a bad omen even the believers of the new faith felt it. Those that could remember started to spiritually cleanse their homes, others prayed and asked for protection, the river's actions had unsettled their souls.

The family moved into the school while the community fixed their house, but even with all their best attempts, Shikulu and Mama's home would never be the same. After a long discussion the community agreed that it was pointless to send a letter informing the siblings of what had transpired, especially as during that time period, letters from Mitondo to the city took at least a month to reach their destination. Finding a working phone to call any of Headmaster's children, to inform them also felt like a pointless mission. Everyone agreed that as the damaged was mostly to property, and there was nothing more that could be done to improve the situation, there was no need to panic the siblings. A decision was made that they would wait for the agreed arrival date to update them on what had happened. The family along with the community could not wait to see Mumba's children, and to hear how Makesa and Kunda were doing, they looked forward to absorbing themselves in the stories the siblings would tell, and they were sure it would be mentally transforming and a good distraction from what had just occurred.

Life Speaks

As the date to return home drew closer, Mumba drove up to Makesa's students' residence on her official graduation day as she had to leave. She had done all that was required of her and completed the aspect of her study that involved practical work. Attaining three years of good grades was not enough to achieve nursing accreditation. Women were required to add a further year to that, on the field for a specified number of hours. It took at least a year on field to prove that they were suitable for the vocation. As Makesa watched her brother park the car, her mood lifted immediately. He was like a beautiful song to her, he always made her feel happy, they had formed an unbreakable bond that came out of their shared responsibilities and the high expectations they had to meet within their family.

Mumba arrived with his wife and Kunda. They had planned to watch a movie together before the date of their departure to Mitondo. For a long time, going to the cinema whenever the chance arose had been an experience the siblings shared. The opportunity to be transported into a magical world of singing, dancing and even comedy was worth the money to them. They had planned to enjoy the city and all its delights before setting off in the morning for the long drive home. Kunda later made a last-minute change to their plan and informed them that he would join them in Mitondo a few days later, as he had matters to attend to in the city.

Through his son's letters to him, Shikulu had become convinced as well as concerned that his sons had allowed themselves to be misled by the freedom fighting movement. He had hoped that Mumba, having returned from the UK would have been immune to the call to fight immediately. But to Shikulu's disappointment Mumba had been persuaded that the fight had to proceed sooner rather than later. The brothers had spoken to many of the people, and they were ready to come together to oust the imperialists. Other countries in support of Black freedom offered guerrilla training for some of the men. There was no stopping the freedom momentum that had begun. Shikulu advised against this; he felt the time was not right as not enough people were psychologically ready. But his sons had become impatient with his inability to include them in his full plan and asked him to outline the entirety of it, so that they could understand his thinking. He always refused believing that his sons lacked the discipline to honour the map to freedom that he had in mind. His plan had been put together through patience and deep contemplation. At some point both his sons had written to him insisting the reasons he had given to wait were not enough for people to continue live in bondage.

This trip home was also an opportunity for Shikulu to impress upon his sons, the need for be patience. Unknown to him his sons had begun to wonder if their father may have become too accustomed to imperialists and was merely hiding behind a story of the long plan to freedom. They had seen what the outsiders were doing and felt it was time to make a move. It was only years later that the country would understand Shikulu's point, when he warned that the imperialists never left anywhere without taking a vital component of the country along with them. By then the country had entered into an agreement that involved paying the imperialists monetary compensation for over 40 years to retake the country from their bloodied hands. It was a desperate glass of water that looked like an ocean to the eyes of a people longing to be free. At the time they felt sure forty years was not all that long when you considered how much they had endured, physically and mentally. They could not have seen or anticipated the economic prison, built to entice, wrapped in a future of poverty & endless war for our people, while the imperialists lands would glisten with the constant drip of wealth being drawn from ours and other lands.

The brothers planned to confront Shikulu. Makesa having watched her father's word proven right over and over, was not in agreement with them. She felt that if Headmaster believed the right thing to do was wait then that is what needed to be done. Aside from the two men there was general unrest in the country, that could not be ignored. Almost everyone was signing up to join the freedom movement in some form or another. They had enough of the belittling, the dehumanising, the savagery, the lies that they brought with them a better life, when anyone with eyes could see that only one type of person was living a better life, while others remained subjugated. They were tired of the killings, of being told that they were not fit to live even on their own land. They were sick of all of it, and despite being at different levels of indoctrination and understanding, their spirits joined together in their common cause, time to overpower this minority oppressor was overdue.

Mumba, his wife, their children and Makesa along with the driver were up and ready to leave by 4am. Suitcases were packed and they headed out to Mitondo. The roads to rural areas were gravelly so cars driving on them had to be in very good condition before any journey, especially the tyres. Departure before sunrise was preferred to be able to manage the inevitable driving hazards that came with long distance trips. Makesa had watched Mumba interact with his wife and children for the whole week she had been living with them, she thought how much she would love a husband who treated her with the respect and kindness he showed his wife. Their home echoed with the sounds of laughter and joy the whole time she spent with them. Her brother was the first to grow their immediate family and they were all proud of him. She imagined that when the realm of souls was handing out life to give to a body, assigning Mumba's soul as the one most suitable for a first born was the perfect choice. It felt like life was laid out for him to simply live it and in turn it rewarded him with his heart's desires.

Western musicals had been flooded into the country and the movie the siblings had watched the day before setting off had been a musical. Mumba having an excellent ear for music had learned some of the songs just by watching the film once, he was also a gifted piano player. He sang a few of the songs he had learned on their journey and added his own spin, the two women in his life preferred it that way, after singing alone, with a smile asked them to join in, insisting it was a fun way to occupy themselves during the long car journey home.

Then the car turned over, to the people in the inside it felt like it rolled over and over for an endless length of time before finally stopping. Makesa had been flung out of the car, she could hear one of the children crying and the next thing she remembered was hearing were two people who did not speak her language run to her aid. She had so much glass pinned in her body, she wondered how she was still alive. They were in the middle of nowhere and she felt sure she would die soon so she began to make peace with death.

One of the women lit a cigarette and told her to smoke it as it would help with her pain, she did not understand and could not remember if she complied. Somehow medical people arrived and moved her from the scene of the accident. From that point on, she believed she was moved alone because she was in such a terrible state, they expected her to die soon and because of that she did not question her separation from everyone. Makesa underwent surgery and remembered long days begging to be allowed to die. She had stopped eating because dying was better than the pain, she was in. Later, when she spoke of her days in hospital, she described glass falling out of her body for days after the accident. Someone from Mitondo came to visit her, after speaking with her, they left distressed. The person called home and explained that Makesa had not been told of Mumba's passing in the crash along with the driver. It remains against the belief system to withhold news of a family member passing from close relatives for too long. The belief is that the person left behind would be bound to suffer ongoing bad energy, as the spirit lost would insist that it be heard. The person left behind would endure days of irritations and encounter minor annoyances or inconvenience until they were freed by the news that a part of them had gone.

People were sent over from Mitondo to deliver news of her brother's death. They were specific people and when you saw them, you knew the nature of the news they were bringing. They also performed rituals believed to bring peace to those grieving, when Makesa saw them, she knew they were bringing sad news. But she was in such pain, added to that her refusal to eat, it took a long time to feel the loss of her best friend. Shikulu's health had also taken a turn for the worse after that news and he was never the same. It was left up to Lupapa to keep everyone and everything together. Years later when she would teach her granddaughter who they were, her granddaughter would watch her cry quiet sad tears that she had held in for years.

A nurse walked up to Makesa and said, "If you don't eat, we will make you, by putting you on a drip", but it means you will stay here longer" Makesa hated the hospital and decided it would be better to convince them as much as possible that she was well enough to be discharged. From then on, she ate enough to convince them that she was not on a slow suicide plan. On one of her many days in hospital the doctor came and informed her that because of the severity of her injuries they could not fix her leg fully, her spine had also been in affected though not damaged, and despite the fact they had done their very best she would walk with a limp for the foreseeable future. He advised her it was likely she would have to become accustomed to living with pain and the final devastation was that from what he could see, it was unlikely she would be able to carry a baby to full term. She had lost her physical health, her nursing career and her hope for a family by the end of that conversation. No one came to check on her after she had been given the news, the marvel of saving her life and the work involved to save her leg was considered triumph enough by the medical staff. There was no concern for her mental state and how she would cope with her drastically transformed life. They drew satisfaction at having saved her life.

While she was in hospital Kunda came in with news he thought would lift her spirits. He had found a woman he claimed to love and wanted to get married straight away. This was surprising to Makesa because he had been seeing someone else prior to this person, a woman from Mitondo. A woman they all agreed was a right fit for him, and importantly she fit the family as well. But because the previous lady he had been engaged to had been wonderful, Makesa assumed the new love interest would be amazing if not better. Besides that, Kunda seemed really happy, he told her how, he had spoken to Shikulu and mama as about his nkobekela (fiancée) and of his plans for Makesa to live with him when she was discharged from hospital. They had both lost their best friends in the family and he felt this would be a good opportunity for them to connect. Kunda promised his sister, he would look after her and had even prepared the room she would sleep in. He assured her that Shikulu was proud and happy with this decision. Kunda was now the eldest son and he had taken charge. Makesa felt grateful for him. Every day that he visited, he shared stories of movies that were showing and though his singing voice was not as good as Mumba's voice, he sang with sadness and passion that she found moving. He told her all the stories that he could think of to keep her connected to what was happening outside the hospital, he tried to do what he thought his brother would have done had he been alive. Kunda had taken over and loss was going to be their bond.

She still had not told him her plan to die quietly. It was also nice to see him and listen to what was happening in someone else's life. When he took her to his home upon her discharge from the hospital, it was a proud moment for both of them. He had recently purchased a house, a modest three bedroom but it was his. All the work he was doing had afforded him the chance to buy a home in which to care for his sister. The morning after she had moved into his home, he went to her room and with a look of excitement told her that he felt time had come for her to meet his new love. He decided that he would take Makesa and his new love to watch a movie. Kunda was clearly enamored, he shared with his sister a conversation he had with his new love about her, and she desperately wanted to help him care for his sister. He added that when he told her what had happened to his siblings, she had wept. Makesa still could not walk which meant for much of the time he had to carry her around the house. His new love whose name was Eneri had told him she wanted to do all those things for Makesa as well. For their upcoming movie day Kunda chose one that had been a massive hit called the Sound of Music.

Saturday came quickly and Kunda helped his sister into her wheelchair. They were on their way to meet Eneri, Kunda pulled up at her house, spoke to her father and she finally came out to the car. When Makesa saw her all she felt was complete unrest, this woman was not better than the woman her brother was dating before, if anything her energy had a heaviness about it, she was certainly not as attractive as her brother's previous love. While for them her looks were not a priority, her brother had called her beautiful repeatedly she had assumed he meant physically. Then there was the question of her energy something about her was not right. But she reminded herself that Kunda was happy, and they needed some joy after what they had all been through, so she maintained the façade of happiness. They loved the movie and for the majority of the drive back home they sang some of the catchy songs. As Mumba was gone only two of them sang, Eneri refused to join in. They loved 'do a deer a female deer' it was easy to learn, it was playful and most of all it was fun, without knowing it Makesa was starting to live a little again. She secretly hoped Eneri would not last in fact because she felt sure Eneri would not, she never shared her concerns that his fiancée felt wrong to her brother.

Later in the week Kunda came home excited burst into her room and declared that on the spur on the moment he had gotten married. He told Makesa that Eneri would be moving into their home that very day, as soon as she had finished packing her belongings from her father's house. Makesa watched and listened in silence, she could see how happy her brother looked and that was enough. When he returned to work a week later, Eneri walked into Makesa's room and with a look of concern asked her sister-in-law how she felt that day? Eneri proceeded to share with her that a life of looking after someone was not what she had planned so early in her marriage. Makesa assured her she did not need looking after and added that it was not her sister-in-law's responsibility to do so. Eneri looked relieved and left.

Lupapa was keen to meet her new daughter-in-law, she had been restless for a very long time after receiving disturbing news about her new daughter-in-law. She had been busy caring for Shikulu who was very unwell having struggled to recover physically from the shock of losing his son added to that he was already in poor health. Lupapa had to remain with him until he was stable enough for her to make the long journey to the city. She had sent Makesa letter a month before, informing them of her intention to visit the newlyweds and her daughter, this gave them at least a week's notice of her arrival.

There was another reason Lupapa was restless and needed to visit her two children, Eneri had come from people unknown to them, and according to tradition and practise, they had sent their people out to find out, about Eneri's people to check for any important issues that they needed to be aware of. In normal times marriage was mostly arranged between people within the vicinity or neighboring communities, family checks were often swift and easy. If the person or their people were worrying or problematic the answer to a request for marriage from the family would be no. This rule applied on both sides; the reasons given had to be compelling the process was not a superficial matter. Eneri's people came from a far region, and travel there was not easy. They expected that making reliable and honest contacts on unknown terrain would made their work harder. By the time their people returned home with news of Eneri's people, Kunda had already married her and sadly the news was dire.

The first thing they discovered was that all neighboring villages refused to marry from Eneri's village. There was what might now be called undiagnosed mental unwellness among almost every single inhabitant in their community. The scale of the problem was such that they were deemed cursed. The people of Mitondo did not need to coax the truth from anyone external to Eneri's village, they were willing and consistent with the message not to marry among her people.

Other communities would wonder if Eneri's village had broken away from important rules that we all observed for the protection and health of our societies. No one wanted to explore the horror that the entire village may have been made up of deviants because no one dared to believe any human would choose that life. What was certain was from the extent of the problem in Eneri's village, more than one person had missed vital teachings. All they knew for sure was that what they had heard and witnessed of Eneri's people alarmed them and Kunda was already married. It was for the best because Kunda was so deeply in love with Eneri that letting him know what they knew and watching him proceed would have been even more heart breaking, Shikulu and Lupapa had been handed a small mercy in that sense.

All they could do was hope that Eneri was the exception, the fact that Kunda was so happy had to be worth something. Those were their hopes, but years of history indicated that their hopes were misplaced. They knew they were wrong but there had been too much pain of late, no one had strength for a fight.

When Lupapa arrived in the city, having carried all manner of harvest from home with her as was tradition, one that Lupapa continued up to the point of her death. Her children never understood how she managed to carry all that food with her on the coach, her tied the food firmly in Chitenge material. It was often an assortment of dried Tilapia, Kapenta (white bait), Sweet potato, Cassava, Chikanda (vegan meat). If it was in season Mama brought it for her children and grandchildren living away from home. There were no less than 4 massive bags with each visit and the food would last for months.

When she arrived, she was horrified to see Makesa looking painfully thin, she looked barely alive. Lupapa saw straight away what Makesa was planning, she tried and failed to change this and one day the answer came to her. She sent for Makesa's young sister Joym from home, and when she arrived gave her the job of pleading with Makesa to eat or at least drink so that she could get better. Joy being tiny having been given this massive task had only her tears to implore Makesa to eat or drink, she did this every day after mama left. Makesa remembers how vulnerable the young child begging her to live looked and she ate a little and drank for her. She promised herself that wherever life took her, and if that road led to wellness, she would repay Joy for her love. Meanwhile Eneri upon seeing a new person in her home, decided it was time to be even more candid. Every morning without fail she would go into Makesa's room and implore her to understand the difficult position she was in.

She explained that she had married a man not fully appreciating that he would come with this much family wanting to live with them. Eneri was already struggling with Makesa being potentially a permanent fixture but now there was Joy. She explained to them how this intrusion on their young marriage had been keeping her up at night and she needed to know when they planned to leave them to live their lives. Eneri included that the more people they had to house and feed meant less for her and her new love. She implored Makesa to leave them before walking out of her room. The days that followed Eneri escalated her abuse, repeating the fact that she had only married her brother on the understanding that his sister did not have long in this world, and asked if Makesa could at least die, as she had been led to believe would happen. For days she would knock on Makesa's door after Kunda left for work and would utter unforgivable things in an attempt to persuade her sister-in-law to leave their home or die, whichever of the two would be fine with her. Some days she would call Makesa selfish and an evil presence in her home, she continued to deny them food and only allowed Joy to eat in the evening when she resumed pretending to be the doting sister-in-law. Makesa began refusing to eat to hasten her passing. But when Eneri felt her words were not producing the desired effect, she rang her father for help.

Throughout Eneri's torture of Makesa, she never told her brother what was happening, Makesa already hated the fact that she was still alive, and on some level her helplessness made her feel as though she deserved to be reminded, that her life was worthless. Eneri was merely reinforcing the voice in her head that wanted death, rather than be assisted with bathing and kept barely living. Years later Eneri confirmed in passing around company and without much thought for the magnitude of her words that prior to her marriage she had been under the impression that Makesa was dying, so her stay with them would be short.

When Eneri's father arrived from the village where he lived since she married, Makesa and Joy discovered he was even more bizarre than she was. Her father unlike Eneri did not have the awareness to hide his peculiarities and made the sisters uncomfortable every time he was around them. Makesa and Joy noticed that he was not as warm as fathers among their people would be with family members. He said little and remained distant the entire week he lived with them the longest conversation he had with anyone in the house was with Makesa when he let himself into her room to give her a verbal dressing down. This was just before his departure, he decided to explain to the Makesa the reason for his visit to his daughter's home. He walked in her room unannounced which in itself was, inappropriate then asked Joy to leave. He sat in silence for what felt like an eternity and when he finally spoke to her, he said "Mayo (mother) how do you feel lying there knowing that you are destroying a young couple's marriage? You are young, why don't you go out and get a job, make a life for yourself rather than just lie there denying this new couple their peace? Our country is doing well, and there are many jobs you can do, a woman your age has no reason to be spending her days in bed, before I leave my daughter, I want you to give me a date when you will be leaving this home. Then I will speak to your brother and let him know that you will be leaving of your own accord and when this would happen. Be sure that I expect to hold you to the date you give. This young couple need to be given a chance to enjoy their marriage." After he had finished speaking, he sat there in her room and refused to leave until she gave him a departure date whether by death or moving out and only then, did he get up and leave her room. At that point walking for Makesa involved pain, moving was painful, living was painful. Yet his man saw fit to spend a long time in her bedroom battering her mind, he insisted that he did not care what happened to her as long as she left his daughter's home.

A few days later Makesa called Joy into her room, she asked Joy to get her the paper with jobs adverts in it, she realised that however much she wanted to be dead, she needed to protect Joy and remove her from what was revealing itself to be an unsafe environment for everyone. Joy brought her the papers and after searching Makesa saw an advert with a countrywide call for people to work in the bank. It read to her like a job she could apply for and do well, but there was a problem, the location of the interview was very far from her home, in another town. After her initial discouragement Makesa decided that it was possible as she remembered that there used to be a bus that was so cheap it was almost free, that bus was intended to facilitate workers commuting to and from their jobs. She thought that perhaps she could use one of those coaches to go for her interview. To be safe she asked Kunda for money for the bus journey and he refused, he said she had no reason or business to be looking for work in her condition, then he asked her if she was unhappy in his home? She explained that it was time to look for work as that would help her get out and about, and maybe aid in her healing. He refused to be a part of that plan, he told her doing so was tantamount to assisting her in killing herself.

On the day of the interview, she stood alone with no money and one bad incident away from giving up entirely. She decided that she would go to the bus depot anyway and see if she could at least get on the free bus to the interview if they still existed. Her return home would have to be a matter she would sort out later, for now getting to the job interview was her objective. Makesa had been increasing her pain medication a little at a time before the interview date, to ensure that when she arrived, her pain would be masked by the medication. She was still not eating the amounts she needed, but it was enough to make Joy worry less. That morning she waited for her brother to get dressed and go to work. She put on the most presentable outfit she had, and without telling anyone where she was going, packed her pain killers picked up her clutches and went for her job interview. Every step she took caused her pain, she had planned her pain killer intake in such a way that the medication was prioritised for the interview, after that she did not know or care very much about what she would do. For now, she accepted that pain would be her reality for the majority of her journey until she needed to numb it. When she finally arrived at the bus depot, she looked everywhere for the free bus, the more she looked at the timetable the more it became apparent that no such a thing existed.

She dropped her clutches to the ground feeling and defeated Makesa started crying, she called out to her brother and to our people not confined in physical bodies to please help her, life had become unbearable and if they could not, she asked that they call her to join them. As she was crying a young man walked up to her, he looked worried and asked why she was upset? His voice was cheerful and friendly, she explained what had happened to her, Makesa told him about her sister-in-law and how she needed to find a job so that she could move out of her brother's house. After listening, he informed her that she was very lucky that morning because he had the money she needed to get there and back. She looked at him, took in his age and the fact he looked like he did not have much himself, he looked similar to street vendors so popular in cities, the ones that sold single cigarettes to the public for a living. She asked him what he would do for money if he gave her his money? He told her not to worry and with a smile gave her the money she needed. When the coach arrived and people started to board, he told her to get in and he would join her later.

The bus was packed and stuffy, she worried with all the people, their baggage and some had chickens in baskets, that when she arrived for the interview, she would not be smelling the best. But she quickly dismissed that thought, she had been very lucky, a stranger had given her money to get to her destination and back. That had to be a sign that everything would be okay. Then she heard a terrible commotion outside the coach. A crowd had surrounded someone, and they were screaming "kabolala" – (thief) she saw some of them beating the person. Her heart skipped because for a moment she thought perhaps it was her angel, and she hoped she was wrong. When some men managed to break up the crowd and end the commotion. She saw her saviour covered in blood. He had tried to steal to make up the money he had given her. The coach was packed and being one of the first to board, there was no way she would have been able to get past all the people ahead of her, if only to give him back his money. All Makesa could do was remain seated, stuck and cry as they took him away.

The journey was long, but they had set out before 7am so she arrived on time. Makesa asked someone for directions to the location of the interview, it was far from the depot but with her clutches she made the walk to the location. When she arrived, she felt extremely hot, not looking as she would have liked but good enough. She hid her clutches somewhere she knew she would still find them after her interview. At the reception point, Makesa was directed to a large hall, where other potential recruits were sitting. She was informed that the first stage of the process would be tests. Years of tests and drilling under Shikulu's watchful eye meant this was not a concern for her. Her fear was the disability that she could not completely mask and what it would mean to them. However, she was there now and with the help of pain killers and her attempts to hide her obvious limp, she felt she could conceal her disability from them for as long as her will remained intact.

When the tests were complete, they were told they would each be called in for face-to-face interviews, the candidates were then advised that they would need to prepare for a long day of interviews. Makesa had no money for food and nowhere to sit and wait till they called her. She sat outside the hall the whole day, not leaving for water or food and not speaking to anyone, the others had managed to make connections and become each other's support systems on the day. Makesa found solitude easy having been trained to walk alone and self-sufficient, in the wake of bullying, being a general outsider and avoiding unnecessary connections with others not aligned with her father's instructions and teachings. For the duration of the day, she did not engage any of the others. It was long past 5pm before she was called in, by then she was very hungry and thirsty, but this was what she had come a long way for, a young man had been assaulted for her to have this chance. Joy had done work a child is not allowed to do in their culture, Shikulu was unwell, and her siblings left at home needed someone to stand beside Kunda so that everything they had been taught could become reality for them. She understood what was at stake and since life insisted that she continue to live, then she had to step into her role. She fought her limp and walked into the room where two white men who sat behind a desk and a white woman beside them taking notes were waiting for her. She remembered that none of the people looked at her as they addressed her, and because she needed to hide her disability this disregard for her humanity was a gift. She answered their questions and when they were finished, she left the room but not before being told to wait until they updated the successful applicants.

Later at night after she had missed her coach back home, along with a number of other people she was called into another large room. Makesa looked around her to understand what it meant for the people called into the room, but it told her nothing, she had not eaten or had water in a very long time. A white man walked in and informed them they had been successful in their interviews and would receive letters in due course to work for Barclays bank. That was the first time she heard the name of the bank hiring them. She was aware of Barclays bank, they all had, and at that time, this was an amazing achievement.

When she arrived home the next day, her brother who had spent the night searching for her felt such relief at seeing her, he could not bring himself to be angry that she had risked her health for a job interview. When she told him she got the job, they were both so happy no one asked her how she had managed to do it. She immediately started to look for a small place for herself and Joy. Kunda was sad that she was planning to leave his home. Makesa thought it may have been healing for him to have his sister near, she sensed that it gave him a pride to be able to look after his older sister when she needed his support. The truth was Kunda had suspected things were not right in his home, but he did a thing that mostly men & some women do, he pretended that if he did not say it, or if he refused to acknowledge it, then the horrible truth in his home would not be real.

Makesa became his accomplice in this destructive illusion because she was too ashamed to tell him that every day after her car accident she had wished for death, she refused to share with not only that her sister in law had been abusive but that each time Eneri or her sadistic father urged her to end her life or leave her brothers home, she secretly agreed with them that her life was not worth living or saving. When she shared the news of her new job and her plans to move out, Kunda only asked her if she had been happy in his home to be freed from the fear he felt, that she had not. Makesa understanding his desperation, told him what he needed to hear. She added that his home had been a place of healing for her, but now she felt well enough to move on to the next chapter of her life. She only told him the truth of the hell that was his home years later when it came time to defend a child who had told the truth, having lived a life of abuse at the hands of Eneri. Even then Makesa only spoke because no one else was willing to face the horror that had become his home.

His name was Mwazanji (what brings you here). He is one of 25 siblings, Grandfather Chombokoto had many wives because he was successful. Mwazanji (Mwazi) chose to stay at his mother's side to protect her and care for her as she was mostly alone. He wanted to be the man of the house as his father was expected to be in many locations pleasing his many wives and making money. Mwazi's people were secretive, protective of their culture and space, to the point they were willing to allow it to die out than open themselves up to outsiders they believed would taint them. They spoke a language so beautiful it sounded like singing and they had no desire to teach it, later one of Mwazi's children would learn it in secret, though having to hide knowing, meant she could not speak it only understand. Mwazi shared two stories with one of his children, she suspected he did that because one was a turning point for him, and the other was as traumatic as it was heart breaking. These incidents became important points that had shaped his life. The first story was the reason he never left his mother's side.

Fiela his mother was cooking outside when two men, who were strangers walked up to their home, that was not unusual people passed through all the time. However, this tribe from the South of the continent, onto Bechuanaland, then Mozambique, and finally the land they settled when movement was forcefully terminated were actively unwelcoming of others and refused share anything with outsiders.

Fiela chose to show kindness to strangers, the men told her they were hungry and had a long journey ahead of them, no one in the community was willing to help them. Fiela was opposed to that thinking, the fact her people refused to take in or help others never sat well with her soul. To be included into Mwazi's people meant a lot was asked a lot of the person wishing to join, some felt they asked too much. Parts of the rituals were dangerous but required as a rule not only for people joining through marriage or other reasons but their children as well. The person would have to doused in sanctified water, using special leaves this would be done in a spiritual person's home. They would then be given a potion to take which made the person very unwell, then the initiate would be placed on what people were informed was a very unsafe piece of wood and left to float for an agreed amount of time before being retrieved. The problem was among other things their river was notorious for having dangerous crocodiles. Finally, they asked that the person denounce their people. If the initiate managed to achieve the earlier steps, the details of which they were never given prior to the process. The final step would be the point many would refuse to continue. Being asked to denounce your people for many was as good as denouncing yourself. Later it became a joke among other communities that the people who agreed to those terms, would have to have been very desperate indeed. They united other tribes in laughing at them. But a large enough number of people accepted the conditions, mostly through marriage and it was enough that the tribe continued to grow in a healthy way.

At the time Fiela agreed to feed the two men, she had just given birth to twins and often thought about the complexities of life's journey. She thought how her own children could one day be lost or alone and in need of a stranger to help them or show them kindness. That is why when no one was looking Fiela shared with others and helped strangers for the sake of her children. That day after feeding the two men and allowing them to sit and rest before setting off, she went into her kitchen to put the food and calabashes away. When she returned, in what felt like a short time, she found her twins had been placed into the boiling pot of food she had left on the charcoal burner and the men gone.

The village Elders were angry with her, everyone was angry, she had been foolish and disregarded the rules designed for everyone's safety, she was not given space to mourn her lost babies because to them she had disgraced herself and had as good as killed her own children. She was told how her error had made their entire community less safe. She was left to cry alone with Mwazi at her side. The twins were his siblings, he mourned them as well. The community wanting to ensure she never again broke safety rules saw to it that her twins were not given a traditional funeral. Lessons had to be learned. Fiela never shared with her son's grandchildren what trauma led to this harsh stance among her people because her grandchildren through Mwazi had become considered outsiders and sharing stories of her people with outsiders was not permitted.

The second pivitol point was Mwazi being teased as he was herding livestock with the other village boys. To them a boy spending as much time as he did with his mother was not normal. The teasing was daily and relentless, he ignored it because he loved his mother and he understood she needed someone's support. But one boy in particular, Shadrack had made it his special activity, every day he committed a large amount of time and effort to verbally abusing Mwazi calling, him all manner of names and the fact Mwazi had never responded, emboldened him to the point he decided one day time had come to escalate his abuse and walked up to Mwazi shoving his head as he worked. It was then that Mwazi had enough, he turned to face Shadrack punching him repeatedly, and because Shadrack was not expecting him to retaliate there was no opportunity to defend himself or fight back. Mwazi beat him unconscious and then he stopped. Shadrack was so badly wounded everyone initially assumed he had been killed. When the matter was escalated not one single Elder including Shadrack's parents felt Mwazi was in the wrong. Everyone had witnessed the abuse, the fact he was still alive was his compensation as far as the Elders were concerned and the matter was left at that. But Mwazi was disturbed, he had wanted to kill Shadrack and the effects of uncontrollable anger terrified him, he made himself a promise from that day that as long as he lived, he would never again succumb to that level of anger. Despite assurances that he had been pushed and rightly reacted, his anger had disturbed him. As he got older, Mwazi became known by all as a kindhearted man who chose daily to walk in love. Those that abused his goodness found that they failed to touch him in the peaceful secure place he resided.

A New Song Is Sung

Mwazi's uncle had come to visit after having lived in the city for a number of years and when he found his nephew working on his father's farm, he mentioned to his brother offhand that a boy his age needed to be in school rather than doing that work. His brother agreed and suggested his uncle take Mwazi to the capital with him when he returned. The uncle's surname was Phiri, not the same as Mwazi's father who was known as Shikulu Nzendo Chombokoto, for reasons not given his uncle had changed his surname name when he moved to the city. When Mwazi left to live with him, his surname changed as well. Uncle Phiri had a son named Shaka, who was albino which made him stand out but not in a negative way. Young children tended to stare at him the first time they met him; many would asked how come he looked different to us. Shaka was always happy to explain to the children why he was them, but something called melanin worked differently in him. It always seemed to make sense to the children, and they would quickly move on. Shaka was a talented musician. A few men he worked with also played musical instruments and on select evenings and weekends, they played music together for pleasure, to unwind and as a distraction from the stresses of their days.

On one music practice day, Kunda brought Makesa along. He was pleased that she had managed to find a job in her condition and felt including her in his musical sessions with work colleagues, may also be a chance for them to relive their fun moments before things changed, when she moved out. Kunda usually drove them both to the week's nominated music

111

rehearsal home, where the music, food and drink created an atmosphere not unlike a party.

Makesa stood beside Kunda as he arranged and discussed music along with Shaka. On that day Shaka had also brought along a friend, a young man who was also helping in their freedom fighting efforts, though he did not work for the mines. He was welcomed because of his support of union workers, Mwazi had become active in politics because most young men his age were. As part of the training, he received to support the cause, Mwazi was given car and motorbike driving lessons to make his outreach work easier. Upon completion he was provided with a motorbike by the grass roots movement. The idea was for him to drive everyone around when there was a need. Mwazi had never been in such environments before so immersing himself in the cause was life affirming for him. His commitment caught the eye of one of the seniors in the movement who assured him that when the party gained majority after the struggle his efforts would not be forgotten. But on this night Mwazi was having fun with his cousin when he saw a young lady that moved his heart.

He asked Shaka if he knew who the lady was, and he did as it was his friend's sister. Shaka knowing Kunda and his protective nature over his family, was concerned, that he would never consent to any of the men whose company he kept approaching his sister in a romantic sense. Shaka asked Mwazi to leave well alone for the sake of peace and encouraged him to focus on the other young ladies that did not come with the added headache that going after Makesa would bring them. But Mwazi wanted Makesa, he decided the best way was to enter their territory in a less conspicuous way. He would join the two men every time they had music practice. This was a good plan except, even though he could carry a tune, Mwazi could not play any instrument, which was a requirement. Shaka was delighted to share this aspect of his life with his brother. When he asked Mwazi what instrument he would like to study, he picked guitar mainly because Shaka played guitar. Mwazi's true intentions were on creating an opportunity to be in the same vicinity as Makesa as much as possible.

Music rehearsal was rotated between homes, however because Kunda was the only one out of the four men with a home, that felt like a home. He tended to host musical days more than the others did. By now Eneri was running a small bar (Shabeen), in a rented room serving mainly local brew while African music blared loudly in the background. Eneri's Shabeen was doing very well. This meant that the men and their practice was not a bother to her. For all her disturbing attributes at home Eneri had a nose for turning people's lascivious needs into money for her. Though she started with selling alcohol, she quickly worked her way down to providing a space for women to meet men for the night for money. Eneri allowed this at a cost to the women for using her establishment to find men. At that point she was making more money than Kunda, however money was never a point of contention for them. Shikulu had raised men who did not fear successful women.

In fact, they encouraged women to participate in the elevation of their surroundings. Most men raised under Shikulu's care went on to marry women who had big dreams themselves and wanted to participate actively in bringing about change in their country. Shikulu's daughters all chose to live, lives focussed on personal advancement, preferring to pursue roles beyond those intended for women only in society at that time. They all believed Shikulu when he told them of the time coming when women's positions in society would look different and they wanted not only to be a part of the change but also to be ready for change.

Every time rehearsal was held at Kunda's house, Mwazi would try to catch Makesa's eye, but she never seemed to notice him. When Mwazi realised that subtlety would not gain him the affection of the woman he liked. He decided to change his approach and speak to her as often as he could. During practice he would attempt to engage her in conversation as soon as she arrived from work. He would speak to her as she hung clothes outside, he would sometimes uncomfortably include her in conversations they were having yet somehow everyone noticed what he was up to except her brother. To Kunda, his sister was disabled and vulnerable and as he had been clear about boundaries with his friends, he continued to operate as normal with the few people he allowed in his home on the understanding that violating his rules would lead to a fight.

Makesa had noticed Mwazi's efforts to engage her, having lived a disciplined life of goals to be met and nothing else the feeling of being gently courted was life affirming. She forgot she limped when she was around him. He was loving to her every time he was with her, she did not feel harassed and found herself looking forward to his attempts at conversation. Makesa admitted later that she thought he was handsome from the moment she laid eyes on him. Aside from getting a job with the bank and having the pleasure of watching Joy be a child, rather than a child carer. Makesa spent much of her free time looking for a suitable place to live, that Kunda would approve of. As a result, Makesa had very few playful moments. Mwazi's attention was unexpected, intoxicating and very welcome. She was twenty-one and the feeling he gave her was wonderful. He made the numerous responsibilities that she carried along with her brother Kunda feel less heavy.

She came alive around him. Other sisters in love at the village had shared with her what it looked and felt like to be courted. But this was the first time anyone had plucked up the courage to speak to her. To Makesa, what she felt for Mwazi was first time in the history of love that people had interacted this way. Headmaster would have personally ended anyone who tried to speak to her in a romantic way while she lived under his care. Her educational advancement in life was his primary concern. Makesa was utterly clueless to the fact that what she felt was natural and not at all unusual, all she knew was it was consuming her. Had she been at home in Mitondo, the women would have

114

shared all of their experiences, so that she could see, that what she was feeling was not new, it was perfectly natural and more common than Makesa would have liked to believe especially as she floated in their love cloud. The new ways had changed them, and unhealthy naivety came as part of the package in the new reality.

Makesa found herself rushing home to see Mwazi on music days. She felt sure that if he loved musicals as she did then it would be confirmation that this was real love. During rehearsal once, Mwazi suggested that she learn to play guitar with him, he had heard her sing and thought her voice was beautiful. He added that if she preferred not to learn she could join him anyway during his lessons. Makesa thought that it would be nice to learn to play guitar and agreed. Shaka understanding what was going on between the two agreed to teach them both and remarkably Kunda did not object. Guitar lessons meant that the two had more time together, years later she would admit to not remembering a single aspect of playing guitar because she used that time to watch Mwazi for confirmation that she was not wrong about him. Later in their slow courtship Mwazi came to her home on a non-rehearsal day and surprised Makesa with news that he had converted to the new faith. He understood the importance of faith to her, and assured Makesa that she was welcome to meet the priest that would confirm this as fact. She agreed and he took her to the church he had been baptised into. The Priest was a man from the new land, a good man, who confirmed everything Mwazi had told her. She was moved by this act of love for her and Mwazi's intention to be with her in love, truth and in spirit.

From that point on there was no turning back, Makesa felt safe enough for him to openly declare his love for her to everyone. First, Mwazi spoke to Kunda, and as expected Kunda was not happy. He drove straight home to ask his sister what was going on and when he saw she was too far gone to dissuade, he spoke to his father about his concerns and asked for their father's intervention. Kunda was so angry he nearly cancelled music days with all his friends, suffice to say it was some time before any of them were welcome in his home again.

Shikulu summoned all of Mwazi's people to visit their home, time had come for the families to meet. Mwazi's people lived a little further out than other tribes, so Shikulu proposed a realistic date to allow them time to prepare. When Shikulu spoke to Lupapa of the news from the city, he was not happy but most of all he was worried.

Shikulu: A young man wants to speak to us about Makesa

Lupapa: That is good news he must love her

Shikulu: I plan to send his people away when they come

Lupapa: Why invite them in the first place only to insult them?

Shikulu: Because I wanted to be sure they had seen her and are not wasting hers and our time

Lupapa: what do you mean Makesa is educated she is doing well, she is desirable?

Shikulu: She has been told she cannot have children and she walks with a limp. What does he want with her?

Lupapa: The same thing men want from women; she is past the age of marriage, and it is time she settled down with someone who loves her.

Shikulu: He is not right, he cannot want a woman who is disabled, and be well within himself, I fear he will abuse her.

Lupapa: That is why we meet them, if we agree he is not right, we will refuse to give our blessing

Shikulu: I do not want his people here, they are stuck in ancient ways, she will be unhappy, and the marriage is unlikely to work

Lupapa: Then when we meet them, we can ask those questions and if we feel she will not be safe, we will withhold our blessing.

The day Mwazi's people were expected was not joyful for Shikulu, he had to be talked out of letting them arrive to a dry reception without food, drink or any of the usual hospitality. Unexpectedly for Mitondo people, the day Mwazi's people arrived was much more dramatic than they had ever known especially in what was now recognised as western influenced times. Mwazi's family arrived in traditional attire and the women walked with pride, some in Mitondo felt they walked in too much pride, maybe even arrogance. Their attire was made from cow skin. The women of their tribe wore had bangles made from elephant tusks, there was only one other tribe in the region with that practice, yet these women had ivory apparel and jewelry on their bodies which was unusual for what had been learned of their ways and culture. Everything on their ears, their nose and their arms were made of ivory. There was always an expectation of a few oddities and unknown facts here and there with these meetings, but these people were almost a complete surprise.

When Headmaster saw their women, he became more concerned for his daughter because of the cultural contrast. He felt, there was no way she would be happy and safe as the differences in customs and behaviour were too vast, and every time the women spoke over their own people or those from Mitondo he shuddered.   That was not how they lived, for them discussion was reflective, calm and long, communicating in that way was what was deemed respectable for them.   He was sure he had not prepared his daughter for life with people such as these.

Everyone was taken aback by the spectacle. In their region humility was a currency but these people arrived with no concern for such matters.   The men existed in a time frame unfamiliar to Shikulu's people. They would not be rushed, pushed, or bullied into meetings. Behaviours that were considered acceptable in Mitondo were ignored by their guests. They moved only when they compelled each other to do so, and worse on several occasions their women were seen smoking and sniffing snuff. They treated all of the hosting village's hospitality as though it was due them. By the end of the first day no one liked them, little did they know that Shikulu Nzendo (Mwazi's father) had put a lot of thought into who he brought along with him, to represent them and help his son succeed in securing marriage to the woman he loved. Shikulu Nzendo had only brought with him the people he felt would integrate well with others, to Makesa's people the only person who came across as approachable and respectful was Mwazi's mother Fiela. Everyone else was what could only be described as an extremity of personalities to any of the people of Mitondo.

Lupapa didn't waste time walking among their guests, feeling their essence in an attempt to understand them. She created an environment where they felt free to speak while she listened. Lupapa discovered that though she could not speak their language they spoke hers, though badly it was more than anyone from her compound had made effort to do for them. In Mitondo, the man desires the woman, as far as Makesa's people were concerned his people were expected to put in the work required, to bridge any communication barriers. Lupapa respected this effort on their part, especially as on a superficial level they had come across conceited. She spoke to Fiela and found her warm and kind, but also worked out quickly that Fiela was not part of the final word in decision making or even an equal partner in her marriage, not in the way Lupapa understood partnership. Lupapa knew that to fully appreciate how her daughter would be treated she would have to get that information from Shikulu Nzendo, Fiela's husband. This would be inappropriate according to custom, so she was forced to take the long route in her investigations.

Shikulu Nzendo was very respectful and clearly a magnetic personality. Despite not wanting to like him, Headmaster found him to be an interesting person. There was a vague story floating around about an entry ritual. But no one had offered any details and Headmaster decided he would ask at the official gathering. Headmaster found his father counterpart to be fair as a human being and when all attention was not on him, he revealed his thoughtful side. This was an important quality for Headmaster to observe in Mwazi's father, the hope was that his son would have similar qualities to the father. Mwazi's people, showing Headmaster signs of being open and reasonable was important especially as having difficult representatives complicated marriage discussions and there was always a danger of a misstep risking the entire process. If a family could not be spoken to at this stage or expected to be a positive contribution into the newlywed's marriage. It was feared that this could be a symbol of how the young couple would be treated and affect their marital longevity. Everyone knew a story of family members being complicit in concealing unacceptable behavior in their child, this was a problem because culturally marriage for also brought both families together therefore there was a spiritual expectation of fairness and honesty, especially from the Elders of both sides. In Mitondo even after divorce the in-law is still called son or daughter by both families. There is a saying that entrenches this 'ubupongoshi tabu pwa' Mother or Father-in-law ties can never be severed once a marriage proceeds.

That is why checks before marriage were considered important, to help both parties fully understand what they were entering into as it was a permanent agreement, for parents on both sides. Mwazi kept a low profile during these discussions, he had to give a good impression and generally it was not advisable to immerse the groom into too much of the festive atmosphere for fear of him making a visible mistake that his family could not remedy. Everyone else was free to enjoy and acquaint themselves with the other family. Elders on both sides quickly familiarised themselves with each other as they would be discussing important matters such as dowry and traditional behaviors to be maintained. In these discussions the bride-to-be's uncles are gods, not the parents. They decide what must be prioritised and preserved, what each family would accept and the starting point for dowry negotiations, which was always eye wateringly high. Those negotiations were a fine art, if the groom's family fought too hard to lower the amount they risked appearing as unfit to care for the bride and her children, worse it could be taken as indication that the man's family did not think highly enough of the woman he claimed to love.

A trick that sons from families unable to meet the costs involved in marriage undertook was come to an agreement as a couple and impregnate the young lady. They knew that the culture prioritised children and impregnating a woman would be considered as dowry fully paid as long as the other side forfeit their rights to the child and future children. A number of men in the area who knew this clause in Mitondo would resort to this strategy, but only if they simply could not afford the dowry. However, this approach came with a warning, the fact that the sum of all your people still meant you could not put together enough dowry was a point of shame. If the man's family came later after marriage with an issue relating to the wife, in which they needed her family's intervention. The precursor sentence would almost always be "For a family that failed to pay dowry you make many requests of our family". This was also the case when the daughter went to complain of ill treatment from her husband or his family. The response from the wife's family would involve a reminder of the fact the man and his people, having failed to meet the bare requirements before marriage, should have been a warning that such a family would end up being long-term problem for them. A man chose the pregnancy route at risk of permanently losing face in future and having in laws disinterested in intervening or help when it was needed.

It was not unknown for men to return to the uncles after marriage to settle the dowry, if only to do away with the sneering that nonpayment caused between the families.

The family that did not haggle down the dowry and paid outright what they were asked, were cause for the future bride to walk with pride as stories of her husband's family loving her so much, they chose not to argue about the first amount they had been asked to pay. In Mitondo the uncles split the money or goods among them. The idea being in the event something should happen, and it was rare, but should something cause the marriage to break down as a result of the wife transgressing, the family were duty bound to return the dowry. The problem had to be something so bad it could not be explained away by wise aunties.

Over the years they had learned that if only one uncle was given the money, in the event they failed to return it or struggled to settle the account in good time, confusion and shame for the compound would ensue, and no one wanted that. Having learned that lesson dowry was always split, as the years went by the mother and father were no longer given a share, and it all went to the uncles. Why tradition changed was not explained.

Pre-marital stages were an important time for the uncles, even before the other family had arrived. People sent out feelers to measure the correct family worth for dowry negotiation purposes, this was done by both families, to ensure they were beginning or responding to negotiations correctly. Makesa's family need not have bothered in Shikulu Nzendo's case, he wanted to show off, the feast they put together in a village that was not theirs, both amazed and impressed. They were so domineering as people that Headmaster failed press them about his reluctance for alcohol to be consumed at celebrations, never mind the debauchery that Mwazi's people indulged in openly and in front the other family to witness. People on both sides looked and felt happy, this coming together of families felt like a sign that the match was a good one. Headmaster was still concerned, even after meeting all of Mwazi's family and realizing they were reasonable, he remained afraid for his daughter.

Before dowry was agreed, Headmaster called the uncles from both families, he shared his fears that Mwazi may not be a good husband to his daughter. He brought up the fact that when they could not have children the marriage would turn abusive for her. Mwazi's uncles stepped in to speak for him, they shared stories of his goodness as a young man, how he supported his mother even when it meant he got bullied, they made constant references to his gentle nature. They were even willing to bring people who were not of their community that would attest to his goodness. Shikulu remained unconvinced. However, he accepted that times had changed, and he did not want to force the young people to marry without his blessing. He asked that the Mwazi's family not pay dowry in exchange for their promise that his daughter would not be abused by them or by their son. He reminded them that they had come to ask for her to join them knowing full well who she was. Then he directed the final instruction to Mwazi, Shikulu reminded him that Makesa was not being thrown out of her family home, nor was she destitute, instead he had come to declare love for her and to take her from a loving home to live with him in harmony. He reiterated that she was loved and wanted always by her family, therefore as her father he did not expect her to be treated as though she had married Mwazi in desperation.

Everyone present was offended, Shikulu Nzendo wanted to pay the dowry, they had come a long way to show that they were a family that women would want to marry into. But Headmaster refused their dowry, as for the uncles from Mitondo their fury was immeasurable, at a later meeting without Headmaster they discussed how he had overstepped and refusing dowry was not his place. Makesa was after all their daughter, but not being able to find a dignified way of resuming the dowry discussions was an obstacle they failed to overcome. They were furious and planned to make their feelings known to Shikulu.

Meanwhile Lupapa had made a discovery, during the time she spent among the women from Shikulu Nzendo's village especially those who lived in close proximity to the negotiating uncles. The women shared freely with her because as far as they were concerned the marriage was as good as agreed. In one of the discussions Lupapa had with them she discovered that children were very important to them, everyone had noticed that they had been surprisingly blasé about enquiries on what happened in their village if a woman could not conceive. Even Makesa's uncles had observed this fact. The truth was traditionally they would insist that the wife allow their family member to have a child with another woman, in the event she was unable to do so. If she refused, they would force the matter anyway and bring a young lady into their martial home. The young lady would be accompanied by an approved aunty or even the mother-in-law who would refuse to leave the marital home and threaten to live with the couple indefinitely, until the young woman brought in was impregnated. The practice worked, and eventually when the young lady was impregnated, everyone except the wife was satisfied. They would then leave the married couple until the next time his family felt it was time for another child. Ultimately children would be produced by all members of their families, in some form or the other. For them the rule of conception applied whether the partner having trouble procreating was male or female.

Hearing about their harsh system was not surprising to Lupapa. They also had their own ways for ensuring continuation of their people. What concerned her was that Mwazi's family were under the impression, that it would not be a problem for Mwazi and Makesa. Someone had told his family that the issue was not that Makesa could not have children, rather, that she should not try to have children. They felt confident that the young people were in enough love that Makesa would want to try for the man she loved. This part of the plan was unknown to Makesa's people and because they had all been charmed by Mwazi's family, they had convinced themselves without confirmation that Mwazi loved their daughter regardless of the likelihood she would have trouble carrying a baby to full term. Besides times were different now and everyone was having to adapt. Lupapa knew that her people were mistaken, but she was also concerned that her daughter had given the groom's family the assurances they held about the couple's ability to have children in future. There was also a very big part of her that wanted her daughter to have children, those ideas and impulses had lived among them for longer than their memories, that would not change overnight. The only person who would have spoken against the idea of Makesa attempting to have children and accuse every one of ignorance, was Shikulu. He would without a doubt have refused to sacrifice his daughter at the altar of tradition. That is why Lupapa decided she would not tell him what she had discovered. He could never understand the reality of not being able to conceive children for a woman in our communities.

Even in their consensual system, where the wife was respectfully asked for permission to allow her husband to procreate with another woman. It was not an easy route to take. The choice of which young lady was always made by the man's family and when they are looking for someone to join the couple, her ability to work well with others in a home was not priority on the list. Fertility cues were all they were concerned with. It was not uncommon that a young lady would bring mayhem into the family because she felt in competition with the wife, or she may simply have had bad character or as was the case for most young ladies chosen, they were just young and immature. The first wife was left to manage the disorder that would inevitably descend in their home. It was then left up to other married women in the community who heard or witnessed problems to give comfort to the first wife. In fact, in Mitondo, it was always the other wives who would step in and either speak firmly to the second wife about her conduct or ask the husband to reinforce respect for his first wife in their home. But truth was even when the young lady was kind and respectful, not a single man ever really thought about the feelings of the wife who could not conceive. Her in-laws did not care; and she was expected to cope because children were more important than her feelings. The married sisterhood were the only thing left to heal her and that is if she shared how she felt at all.

As much as Mwazi loved Makesa and Lupapa believed he did, the inability to conceive children not only came with unavoidable hell from the extended family, but it would also invariably cause friction between the married pair. As a young couple they could not imagine the strain that infertility brought until they were living it. Lupapa could not allow that horror to happen to her daughter, and she decided that she would encourage Makesa to continue with the lie that everything would be fine. Then she would use every power she had to help her through her pregnancy. Lupapa reasoned that even if her daughter had just one child, it would be better than none. She may have convinced herself that one child would be enough for everyone, in practise she knew no family among their people would accept one child. She decided not to get ahead of herself, the first step was to support and help her daughter with the first child. Later that day Lupapa wrote to Makesa telling her that when she was expecting and she was sure the baby had taken hold, she was to call her. Lupapa promised that she would be with Makesa from the third trimester until a year after the birth personally caring for her and the baby.

When everything was finally agreed between the families all that was left to do was to get married. By now Mwazi was working full time for a local political party and having been given a car by the leadership for his outreach work it meant he could give Makesa his motorbike to use. Mwazi taught her how to drive his motorbike, he decided this would save her the long uncomfortable journey to work by bus, on the days Kunda could not give her a lift. Having been on the motorbike with him several times she was very excited and learned to operate it in no time. The motorbike gave her freedom, but as they were not quite at the stage where women wore trousers frequently,

Makesa had to make do with thick tights and a strategically placed cloth around her thigh area to maintain modesty.

When it came time for their church wedding Makesa selected a simple pencil Ivory dress and veil, Mwazi wore a plain black suit. The two witnesses were Kunda and Shaka. The Priest was a young man from Ireland, and theirs was the first marriage he had officiated. Fr Jude was friendly and excited about doing the work of the Lord. He had spent some time with the young couple during pre-marital classes and a friendship had ensued, it was a friendship insofar as anyone could be friends with a person who would only ever exist to them, in a professional capacity. Navigating such relationships was not alien, the couple had both grown up in environments where, someone's position within society or community remained at the forefront of the mind. However friendly or informal people in certain positions appeared, there remained internalised understanding in everybody that specific people maintained their seniority whatever the occasion. Elders, Chiefs, community medical people, aunties, uncles, mother or father, are examples of senior positions that took no time off in formal or social settings. Children had stories of that one uncle or aunty who was playful and whilst this was welcomed by the very same children, most Elders tended not to be playful to maintain the respectability of their senior positions.

Their friendship with Fr Jude was viewed through a similar lens, they had taken him for tours around the city and he promised that when they married, he would make regular home visits to their house. Being the first marriage, he had given a blessing he felt spiritually bound to making sure their marriage remained intact. Not many people would commit to checking in on a couple for over fifty years, but he did. There are many men and women who have no business going into the vocation that is the clergy. But this man was true to his calling.

On the wedding day, Makesa arrived with Kunda, while Shaka drove Mwazi to the chapel. Their church wedding was unlike any of the cultural weddings, which were open to everyone. Every story told going back as far as they could remember, applied the principle that during wedding and funeral celebrations there was no such thing a stranger. Everyone was welcome at those events. During weddings the air would be filled with music, local musicians would start playing long before any guests arrived, because music was central to creating and maintaining the mood. Every dancer, singer and musician among them would step up and offer to add their talents to the joyful occasion. There were always a variety of drums and the sound each produced was unique to that drum. There were many factors that determined the overall sound produced such as the animal skin used, how the skin was dried and applied onto the wood, all those things came together to produce a unique sound of its own. Makers of ingoma (drums) knew what they wanted from a drum before putting one together. When it came time to inspire dancing, drummers would select specific ingoma, the sounds of which were designed to make even those that lacked the dancing gift, to get up and move to the rhythm. Drums were the main instruments used because of the powerful effect they had on the spirit, body and mind each time they were played.

There would be dancers from both families and from the wider community, each side would put forward their best dancers to represent their family. Whilst the best dancers were given gifts to recognise their skill for other festivals, during weddings it was more about the honor of having out danced everyone, including all the other family's dancers. This was done in good humor and families happily recognised when they had lost a dance contest, and graciously celebrated the winner. Some would even promise gifts to opposing dancers if their skill was amazing enough. All dancers were aware that their movements had to work in concert with the drums and those that were particularly gifted, were known to inspire drummers to switch rhythms in creative ways, to test the dancer's ability to keep up. Most struggled to keep up successfully with the frequent rhythm changes. Those that managed, knew they had set a new standard when all the drummers had nothing left in them to challenge the dancer. It was not unknown for drummers to throw their instruments at the victorious dancer. This action was considered high praise.

Singing was always inclusive though starting and leading the songs was assigned to those recognised as being good singers. The intention was always for everyone to join in.

Some of the songs required a response and sometimes when a female married guest felt that she needed to shame her in-laws, she would pay singers to stand next to the family in question and start singing songs expressing how difficult being their daughter in law could be, one such song went as follows:

Mwangamba, Mwangamba, mwa ndekako x2 and everyone would respond in song singing the same words, (Talk about me all you want, but allow me to rest from time-to-time x2)

The family would be in no doubt the song requested was for their benefit and each time they pretended not to notice. Suffice to say they did not sing along. This song would go on until an obviously amused Elder would decide the targeted family had had enough. There was always a chance for rebuttal, and on occasion, another daughter in law would pay singers to sing how wonderful her in-laws were and to emphasis the point, she may make a show of being seen paying a young person to dance for her in-laws. Whilst a rebuttal was known to happen, it was never enough, as accusations of being unkind to daughter in laws were always taken seriously. People present would question why another woman would choose to potentially contribute to her sister's misery in a family by contradicting her experience. Often the cries of a distressed daughter-in-law were taken seriously as lying about that would only lead to a harder life for the woman. To counter a song of a wife's distress was seen as shameless sucking up, and not good form. For those reasons the counter song would deliberately receive lethargic responses from the wider wedding party. A wise daughter-in-law did nothing after her sister in marriage spoke against their husband's people, because though she may well be happy it was not for her to decide that the care she received was universal.

The food at weddings was endless. There would be spit roasts of goats and cows turning continuously, chickens roasting, fresh and dry fish, the fresh fish would be served first, sweet potatoes, sugar cane, roasted ground nuts, pounded nuts, Rape pronounced Repu which are delicious local greens, all cultural delights were provided. Everyone was fed till they could eat no more and even then; the eating did not stop. Children had fruits juices sourced from surrounding fruit, sometimes they used straws made from a special tree balk to suck juice from the fruit, most of the fruit would be very ripe and soft enough to squeeze aiding with suction of the fruits juice.

The wedding Chibuku used will have been brewing for months before the date, other extra potent beer would be brought out on those days as well. Children were allowed a cup of Chibuku with sugar cane juice added, there were non-alcoholic versions but at weddings young people of age were permitted to drink alcohol.

No one who attended these weddings ever forgot them, even after the tenth wedding, stories would be told about each individual day. Something always happened to set each wedding apart.

There was always a funny thing that occurred, an Elder doing something unacceptable, someone embarrassing themself, even delightful memories such as the groom and brides' love for each other or children dancing that blew everyone away. Life happened at people's weddings, and they were all stored in memory. Their weddings were like no other as far as they were concerned, no one could match the joy that consumed everybody on those days. The Chieftain rarely attended and when they did,

129

it was only to show their faces, have one drink, if that and then they would return to their homes. The nature of their role meant that they anticipated accusations of showing special preference to one over the other, that was only one of a number of issues they had to take into consideration before attending social events. Their safety was a factor, there was no guarantee that a person who may have felt unfairly treated during the justice process, would not attempt to take matters into their hands through the food or drink at a wedding.

Makesa and Mwazi's at a chapel which consisted only of five people including the bride, groom and Priest was unusual. But times were changing. On Mwazi and Makesa's day there was a simple mass and in no time the two were married twice. The first marriage being the coming together of families and reaching an agreement between them. This was done in the absence of Makesa as she could not attend at the time. Her absence was not a problem as the importance of that celebration was more to do with the union between the families. Though the church ceremony was second, it was necessary for record keeping. One of the many changes to traditions and established cultures was that their marriages were now required to be recorded by the Boma (state), every couple needed to go through the new channels to be deemed acceptably married by the invaders. Those channels were either through the church or the local authority. After they had finished speaking to the Priest, he called Mwazi aside and asked him where he was taking with new bride? Mwazi replied that they would be going straight to home. The Priest suggested he take his wife somewhere nice first, which was fortunate for Mwazi because he had not thought of doing that. He took his bride first to a café where they had bottled coke and ate local meat pies, then he took her to the cinema. By the end of their day when he looked at her, not only did he feel like a lucky man, but he was also relieved because she seemed very happy that the day, he had planned very quickly from church had gone well.

When they arrived at his two-bed house, it was the first time she had ever been there, Makesa was taken aback at how basic it was, when she inspected further, she found he only had one of every piece of cutlery, fortunately the house was clean. She decided that the first thing they needed to do was furnish their home. Makesa would find out later the real reason he only had enough items in his home for one person.

At the beginning of their work week, Makesa went by motorbike to the bank, and Mwazi drove to his place of work, it felt like they had always lived together.

Eneri and Kunda were doing very well financially, Eneri's businesses were thriving. She had opened two local bars at this point, having started from a single room Shabeen her rise in the business world was impressive. She took her customer service seriously and often drove men home after she parted them from their money in her establishments. Eneri owned a white pickup van, the open back area was where the men would sit as she dropped them off home one by one. She was known for driving with a bottle of beer between her thighs, taking swigs from the bottle as she drove. Up until the day she lost her limbs to diabetes, Eneri defiantly drank alcohol while driving everywhere.

Eneri had become much more pleasant since Makesa had moved out of her home. She never joined their sibling outings, preferring to keep herself busy making money. She was known to beat men and women up, for owing her money and on more than one occasion had attempted to run over people with her van. Her dangerous behaviour was accepted as being part of what could be expected for someone in the industry she worked. No one questioned her mental stability.

In their early marital days Makesa spoke to Mwazi to ensure they were in agreement on plans for their future together. Both were in sync on what future direction to take, and they put together a basic financial plan that also allowed for life's unexpected turns.

They began with furnishing their home as Makesa requested. She loved that part of their planning; at the same time, they began saving for their own car, as they felt the time was right to start trying for a child. They agreed that it would not be practical or safe for Makesa to continue using a motorbike when she fell pregnant. She loved that he enjoyed hearing her ideas, he loved music just as much as she did and they went to the movies whenever they got a chance, and money was permitting.

Making Room For New Life

One evening when she arrived home on her motorbike after work just as she had done for the last eight months, she saw Mwazi sitting outside with a woman she thought was striking and looked similar enough to her husband for her to conclude she was one of his sisters. Makesa had not met all his family and was only familiar with her father and mother-in-law. Her husband looked very happy as Makesa approached them, they were speaking their language which she could not understand, but she got the gist of what they were saying for the most part. With her most cheerful voice and best smile, Makesa said "Mulamu" (Sister or brother-in-law). The beautiful woman smiled back but not quite, Makesa tried to shake the feeling the woman did not like her, why would she not? They had never met. Makesa maintained her friendly demeanor and with a smile asked if their guest had been offered any food?

The woman replied "My brother has already seen to providing me with food" she said that with the smile that was not quite a smile. Embarrassed by the lack of warmth she was receiving Makesa proceeded to go into the house and begin making dinner. It had become something of a tradition that when they arrived home from work, they cooked together while sharing stories of the day they had both had. But his sister had come to visit, and Makesa was happy to make dinner alone, she hoped her meal would please her sister-in-law. Feeling proud of having had the foresight to purchase cutlery and plates for special occasions, she beavered away putting together a special meal. She may not win her in-law over, but she would ensure that whatever was said about her from that point on would not be that she had not been welcoming or hospitable in well-kept home. His sister would see that Mwazi was very well taken care off by his wife.

When food was ready and despite the fact she was exhausted after having come home from work to start making dinner alone on a hot day. She managed to plaster her best smile on and went outside to invite them both in for dinner. Somehow the sister-in-law looked even more intimidating than their initial meeting, so much so she had to fight the urge to do a deep curtsy as she came out to invite them in. This gesture of respect would look to an observer as though the person was kneeling all the way to the floor or ground. But the person stopped short of doing so before their shins make contact with the ground. It was an action reserved only for Elders, and there is an art to it, dipping too low that you were kneeling would be seen as excessive and most Elders would encourage the young person to rise. The correct way tested the thigh muscles. It was rare that people not accustomed to this action got it right the first time. But Elders were forgiving as trying was better than not. Most young men and women would have been greeting Elders in this way from childhood, the only time anyone would mention how hard it was to get right was when outsiders attempted to replicate the act. As children, learning to kneel correctly for Elders was part of their training, a gentle tap on the lower back was instruction that you had not bent low enough and only the aunties were permitted to give this instruction. When young people were summoned into the presence of Elders, they knew not to rise fully unless their greeting was received and even then, hands clasped together, eyes lowered but still able to look at the Elders.

Makesa looked at her sister-in-law and asked " mulamu what name shall I call you", the woman replied "Nineo Viyoleti " (Iam Viyoleti), this time no smile was attempted by sister-in-law. She got up and walked straight to her room, presumably because she had already explained that Mwazi had addressed her hunger needs. However according to Makesa's culture it was rude of her to retire to her room just as they sat down to eat. Makesa and Mwazi ate off the fancy plates and drank from the fancy glasses alone, what confused Makesa even more was that he appeared oblivious to his sister's obvious disapproval of his wife. That night there was no warm checking in on each other's day. She asked Mwazi if he had known his sister was coming and he replied that he did not. On both sides, family are not obligated to inform relatives when they plan to visit and asking how long they would stay, remains out of the question. Even with knowing these rules Makesa had become accustomed to the open communication with her family in all matters, especially before any of them came to visit, this was the case even when she lived with Kunda, they were always made aware of the impending visit beforehand.

However, this was her husband's sister and she had to remain silent, should word go back to his family that Viy had been in anyway slighted by Makesa there would be uproar. The truth was Viy was rude and at the point Makesa was meeting her, she had four children by three husbands. Whilst another woman would allow the judgements of others to make her squirm or walk in shame, Viy freely discussed the parental status of her children something about her terrified even the most inappropriate inquisitor. The last time Viy was questioned as to why a fairly young woman had had three ex-husbands, she responded that she had loved those men for a time and left when she no longer felt the same. Viy would then move the conversation along as for her that was the end of the matter. No one dared attempt a follow up question and since Shikulu Nzendo thought she was hilarious, no one could rein her in.

That evening Viy walked up to Makesa as she was cleaning the kitchen and out of nowhere said "I had been told that my brother had married a cripple and came and see for myself" Makesa was stunned at being called such a derogatory term, especially as no one around her ever discussed her physical condition. She did not respond, she refused to respond to what was an obvious insult and carried on with her cleanings as though Viy had not spoken to her. That night as they lay in bed, she told Mwazi what Viy had called her. He was upset and assured his wife that he would speak to his sister about her behavior. The next morning, Viy was still in her room when they left, and he decided it could wait until he returned from work. Makesa normally loved her job despite the obvious racial discrimination within the workplace, but that day she struggled to work without distraction. Her sister-in-law's hostility was confusing for her, the helplessness she felt was what made the situation worse. What she had not shared with anyone including her husband was that by then she was expecting, she had counted four months, she wanted to avoid hostility and unhealthy environments, until time came for her mother to traditionally point her out as a pregnant woman. They believed this practice protected the expectant mother from miscarriage or prevent someone unhappy with the wonderful news sending harm on a spiritual level and interfering with the pregnancy. After the ceremony of pointing out a pregnancy, it was then considered safe to confirm that a woman was expecting but only in response to those that asked directly. Makesa wanted to keep her environment serene and loving, but it appeared her sister-in-law had other plans, she found this unsettled her. By the end of the day, she had convinced herself that the love of her life would sort any issues out with his sister and even if they would never be friends, civility would also be acceptable to her.

When Makesa arrived home, she found the kitchen a total mess, someone had clearly been cooking and left all the dirty dishes in the sink, worktops were filthy and had she checked the bathroom, she would have found that the bathtub had been used and the dirty water left undrained. Mwazi having arrived home first, had quickly addressed that issue before his wife saw it. Makesa could not understand how one person could make such a mess. Viy walked past her in the kitchen and went outside without so much as a greeting. Makesa looked for her husband, and when she found him asked him why his sister had left such a mess in the house? He assured her that he had spoken to Viy, and it would not happen again. Yet still the behaviour left Makesa confused, they did not have cleaners and Viy appeared to not be accustomed to cleaning up after herself. Her brother claimed she had other people clean for her at home, but the level of mess created by one person, coupled with the lack of attempt at doing any cleaning after herself was not behaviour Makesa could understand. Makesa decided to apply a saying in Mitondo that went 'lie down and play dead this storm is not here to stay', she also planned to kill Viy with love, unfortunately she was not prepared for how calculating and determined her sister-in-law would be to foster confusion in their home.

A car pulled up in their driveway, and a beaming Viy rang outside where a handsome man stepped out and greeted her. He was not tall, but Viy was short herself. It was the first time Makesa had seen her smile, a real smile from her heart. This handsome and assertive man walked up to them and introduced himself as Dingiswayo, a beaming Viy stood beside him. Makesa thought how good it was that he looked mentally and physically stable because, he would need to be with the person his heart had chosen to love. They invited him into their home, Makesa had been in the process of cleaning the house and would have preferred to have been better prepared for their guest's arrival. But they were clearly living in Viy's world at that moment, she reminded herself that it would not be for long and allowed herself to indulge the bad behavior. Makesa went in the kitchen to prepare a meal for their guest and was later joined by Mwazi, she felt for him as he rarely had a chance to spend time with his family, she suggested he go and sit with his sister and her new beau. But he wanted to stay and help her, he was aware that Viy had been hurtful to here, and Mwazi wanted to be around her as a form of physical comfort and confirmation that he was there for her first. When they sat down to eat, Makesa prepared a hand washing bowl and towel for the guest. When everyone had washed their hands, she went to the kitchen washed hers and joined the family. She hoped they would notice her lovely dinner set and Dingi being a gentleman not only noticed but congratulated her on her lovely home. She decided then he was a nice man. Then something surprising happened, Viy looked at her and said "Mulamu we will be going to Mozambique to start a new life because Ba Dingi has found a very lucrative job opportunity there and would like me and the children to join him.

Dingi proceeded to share how he planned to make a lot of money in Mozambique, but the plan was thin on detail. A point that was not missed by both Mwazi and Makesa, but they did not press him, it was not their business and besides the man seemed very sure of himself. He planned to take Viy to her people first where they would get married and then he would go ahead of her and the children to Mozambique to prepare a home for her to join him. It sounded like a good plan, and everyone was relieved that Viy's mood had improved. So much so that an already apprehensive Mwazi decided without fully acknowledging it that perhaps they would be no need to address the matter of his sister's offensive words to his wife. That unconscious decision was obviously nothing to do with Viy being too much of a handful, a total nightmare in fact that would rain hell on all of them if she felt attacked. He was not worried at all that Viy would be unrepentant after he confronted her. No Mwazi did not think or tell himself any of those things, he did not even acknowledge that in choosing not to speak to Viy he was betraying his wife. If he looked at things in that way, he would have had to accept that the right thing to do was to set clear boundaries with his sister, but that would have involved doing the unthinkable and possibly having to explain to her that if she did not respect his wife, he would ask her to leave until she respected their boundaries. Instead after clearing up, they saw Dingi off as he would not be staying the night in their home before his sister was married to him. That was simply a formality, anyone who saw them could tell they were already sexually active, but tradition was tradition. That night Makesa went to bed with the understanding her husband had addressed the distressing incident she had with Viy earlier and he went to bed hoping it would all work itself out by morning.

The following day was a Friday and every Friday evening, the couple attended training held by their local Priest. The Priest had decided that he wanted them trained as his primary support couple in the marriage counselling program, he planned to implement. He wanted the couple well versed in administering counselling that was in line with church doctrine. They were honoured by the trust that their Priest had in them, but for a while after the decision had been made to choose them, other couples that had been married longer felt snubbed. In the end the decision to select a newly married couple as support marriage counsellors proved to be the right one.

Friday counselling training would go on well into the night, so the two had an agreement that Saturday morning was a day of recovery before attending other social church activities. There were a several male and female segregated gatherings within their church, which were designed for people of the faith to spend time with others of like mind. The new Priest had established these groups as he was determined to involve the people of the country because when he arrived, he had found active racial segregation within the church, that did not sit well with him. Black people within the congregation were not included in any church activities. He spoke separately to the Caucasian congregation, in an attempt to end that system. But Fr Jude was met with resistance. He decided that he would have to establish new activities and include Black congregants. He planned to have Black leaders at the forefront of all his new initiatives. It was not long before there was not a single Caucasian parishioner left at his church, that did not deter him. He only shared his disappointment at the extreme response from the parishioners with the Mwazi and Makesa years later, at the time however he planned to do the Lord's work in light and truth.

After Makesa and Mwazi returned home from training, they found the house filthy yet again and having eaten at the church there was some relief that all they had to do was clean up after their disrespectful guest. This time Makesa decided that the current arrangement with her husband's family was not how she planned to live, moving forward and made a mental note to speak with him when their unpleasant guest left. She was aware that Viy would return at some point and had no plans to keep biting her tongue each time her sister-in-law came to visit. On their relaxation morning off, they were woken by loud noises coming from the kitchen. Makesa after wiping her face went to see what the commotion was all about. She found her sister-in-law packing the contents of their kitchen. Makesa asked her what she was doing and Viy replied that she was taking the things with her as she was leaving later that day. That was where Makesa drew the line, those items had been selected by her for her home, they gave her joy, and no one was going to take her things without so much as a by your leave? She asked Viy to stop packing her things immediately. Viy looked at her and said, "This is my brother's home, he is obligated to take care for me and when I visit him, I take what I want". Makesa replied "That may have been the case when he was a single man, it does not apply now. If you want money to go and buy yourself kitchen utensils, we would be happy to give it to you, but you may not take these things" she said this with a smile hoping that, would be enough to convince her very intimidating sister-in-law that she meant for the matter to end peacefully. Then all of a sudden Viy shifted the energy in the room, looked at Makesa with a passive face, then as if in slow motion and with a wicked smile asked "Did he tell you that he was supposed to marry my friend?", at that Makesa decided she was no longer willing to playing her games and replied "Mulamu this is about my kitchen utensils", Viy gave her a long stare and said, "You will not last in this home I promise you that" and she walked off. By now Makesa was shaking, she had been insulted and disrespected in her own home, in what tribe was this behavior was acceptable? She went to their room and told her husband what happened, and she insisted he speak to his sister as this was a step too far.

Mwazi got up reluctantly, he wondered why Viy could not contain herself. He had felt trapped for years because like everyone, he chose to indulge Viy mainly because she was so willingly contentious, after years of her noise it felt easier to simply let her have her way. Now she had left him no choice but to speak to her and truth be told he did not want to. He got dressed, knocked on her bedroom door and asked to have a word with her in the living room. When she entered Makesa stood by the door peaking and listening through the crack to hear what would transpire. Mwazi asked Viy if she had slept well, and she confirmed that she had. He proceeded to ask about the words she directed at his wife on her first day specifically. He asked why she used derogatory language about Makesa's disability? She was so shocked that he had confronted her, she sat in silence, Mwazi then asked why that morning she told Makesa he had planned to marry another woman? This time she smiled and looked down but still gave no response. There was something about him that morning that he was not aware of, and she could not understand, but whatever it was rendered her speechless for what might have been the first time in her life. She did not want to fight or argue with her brother, instead she chose to sit in silence. And because she was still Viy, she would not apologise or take anything back. He reaffirmed that he loved his wife and he wanted Viy to speak to his wife with respect in future. They sat in silence for a while, then Mwazi asked if she wanted money to buy things for her home, she declined, they sat for a while longer till she asked him if she had his permission to go and finish packing.

Dingi arrived on time to pick Viy up and they embarked on the long drive to her family home. Before he had arrived Viy had spent much of the day outside in the sun sitting on the ubutanda (African grass woven mat), where her brother joined her for a spell. When Dingi arrived Mwazi gave the couple some private time to speak. She was then left alone for a while as Dingi loaded the car with her luggage and just as Mwazi had witnessed before she ran to meet him at his car when the last bag was packed, and it was time to leave. Where another woman would have waited to be informed that time had come to leave, Viy followed her heart and run to the current love of her life. Meanwhile Dingi had completely charmed Makesa. He made sure to ask her permission to enter their home, and take Viy's bags and of course she agreed, once the bags were in the car and his impatient lover had run to him, they drove off, leaving Makesa and her husband to breathe a deep sigh of relief.

Kunda received news that Mumba's third child, his only daughter had passed away, what happened exactly was unclear. But word came back that his brother's widow had never fully recovered from the car accident, whether the child's death was an accident or by natural cause was not clear. But when Makesa heard that her late brother's daughter had passed away she was inconsolable. She rang Kunda and told him that if Mumba's late wife was unable to properly care for the remaining two children and something happened to them as well, the sin would be theirs. Kunda agreed that they needed to speak to their sister-in-law and enquire if she was unwell as they had been told, he would suggest that Shikulu's people be given permission to assist her with the boys, while she focused on getting better. But first, they needed to go to Mitondo to request permission from Shikulu before they could act. The siblings agreed a date to return home. By then Kunda could see that his sister was expecting but said nothing and before long it was time to head home and speak to Shikulu. When they got there, they found their people in mourning, the family were devastated at the news of a lost child.

Shikulu in particular had taken the news very badly, anyone could see by looking at him that he did not have long on Earth. Mumba's wife was there, and she was a shell of herself, even her tears looked exhausted, and everyone was worried for the future of the two boys in her care. Kunda humbly led the discussion to adopt the remaining two children from her, and to their surprise their sister-in-law did not fight them or even object. She claimed that she actually wanted his children brought up by them, her people also consented to the new arrangement. Kunda having offered to care for the children assured everyone that he was doing very well financially, and the children would want for nothing. He was convincing enough that they felt secure knowing the children would be in good hands with him. They all remembered how he had stepped up and helped nurse his sister back to life from the brink of death, trusting him came easily as a result.

At 4 am just before the first sign of light, Lupapa with a clay jar filled with water in arms walked up to Makesa's room. The night before Mwazi had been asked to stay late with the men and stay away from the marital bedroom. He had been given the reasons why, and with Lupapa assured that Makesa was alone she prepared for the ritual. The door was unlocked because she expected her husband to return to their room. Lupapa knocked on the door and listened as Makesa stirred and slowly rose to open the door. As she was doing that Lupapa filled her mouth with the contents of the jar, she knocked again and on hearing that her daughter was closer to the door, Lupapa prepared her lungs opened the door and sprayed the contents of her mouth on her daughter's face as soon as she saw her, then said "I point you out as expecting and from this day on, it is safe to confirm only to those who ask that you are expecting." Most expectant mothers laugh when this happens, they knew the ritual, what they never knew is the day it got done because the element of surprise is part of the process.

Their deceased brother's wife was not alone in struggling to recover from the trauma of the accident, her sons were having trouble as well. She never shared with Makesa, what had happened to her during or after the car crash, she sealed all the horror in her heart. Makesa could not remember seeing her sister-in-law or her brother, she did not remember seeing anyone on the day of the accident all she remembered was being flung far from the car and the pain she felt. Both women and the children shared the horror of that day in common. Where her sister struggled to move on Makesa had built a wall around that day to protect her from the pain and death. She envied her sister-in-law for living the truth of what had happened rather than blocking it. Her sister-in-law had allowed herself the opportunity to acknowledge her lose and grieve.

After obtaining their sister-in-law's consent for Kunda to raise the boys, it was agreed that they would leave with him as soon as he returned to the city. Kunda felt confident that Eneri would understand why he needed to care for his brother's children and never gave it another thought.

Before they left to head home, Shikulu called Makesa to speak with her, she found him in the communal area waiting for her and when he saw her, he looked at her stomach and asked "Mayo ninshi mwachilitila ifi?" - "Mother why have you done this"? She said nothing, he pressed "What about what the doctors told you, for your own good"? She remained silent and even as he spoke, he knew it was pointless, the deed was done and all he could do was give her his blessing so that she could move forward with that at least. He asked her to come closer and said, "I bless you and put into the world that you will deliver this baby without any problems, I declare that you and the baby will be well." She thanked him and left to prepare for the long journey back home. Before leaving home, she asked for Joy to join her in a couple of months, as she meant to keep the promise she had made to her sister. Another reason for asking her young sister to join their home was because it would mean less children for

Shikulu and Mama to care for. Makesa's parents agreed to this arrangement.

When she got home, she was happy to see her love and swiftly fell into their normal life routine. At work they showed no interest in her condition, nor did she wish to share her joyful news with them, especially in light of their lack of interest in her general welfare on a normal day. She thought about how the women from the invader's countries would make such a fuss when they were on their period or pregnant. Makesa had watched them pampered and fussed over to the point of being ridiculous. It was orchestrated and intended to emphasis the fact that those women were considered more feminine than indigenous women. In truth no self-respecting Black woman would have subjected herself to such a spectacle.

There were days Black people would laugh at the foolishness they witnessed in their places of work. The stories medical people would share of the undignified conduct to convince Africans that behaving not dissimilar to an ill-mannered child equated to superiority made them shake their heads in dismay. Makesa had long accepted that she was not perceived as human by them, she knew full well that pulling the same stunts as her white colleagues would have resulted in her dismissal, that was not to say she would have wanted to behave in that way.

Indigenous people were fed a daily diet of their superiority, they were yet to witness this higher level of human existence, they had seen numerous occasions of human mental and physical fragility, and it appeared their only form of superiority was looking down their noses at other human's ways of life.

When Mumba was alive, he had shared with Makesa that one of their tricks was to belittle and call other ideas foolish while they stole them and eventually claimed those thoughts, crafts, cultures, skills, medicines as theirs. By now a significant number of Indigenous people had begun to believe that their inferiority was true. Many kept silent, listened, and looked down when the invaders talked down to them, some shared their experiences and laughed as form of comfort or an attempt at holding on to their sanity. Sadly, too many were broken by the experience.

Their negative experiences at work meant that despite having a high-risk pregnancy Makesa would work throughout her pregnancy and only planned to take the absolute minimum time off after their baby's arrival. Makesa worked through to the end of the third trimester, something her doctor had advised against, but she also wanted to have everything. She wanted the job that gave her personal satisfaction, her marriage and the baby that would fulfil her motherly instincts while also keeping her promise to Mwazi's family. When Mwazi's people were given news of a baby on the way, they were delighted. His aunties paid them a visit to them without warning because culturally Makesa was past ready to be initiated into their tribe. The aunties were lovely and respectful, unlike Viy they were also very clean people with impeccable manners. For the duration of the week Makesa could not find a bad word to say about them. However, they had a reason for making the visit, all matters concerning her initiation were directed at Mwazi, who was expected to explain to his wife. They let him know that they needed an answer before they left to give them time to prepare when they returned home. In true Mwazi fashion he waited till the last minute to tell his wife what was required of her. He told his wife the evening before they left that his people needed her to undergo the ceremony before she had the baby to integrate her fully. The same process would be repeated when the baby was born. Makesa was apprehensive, she was already taking heavy risks being pregnant and working full time, what if the rituals they asked her to undergo were the final straw on her body? The journey to his people was long enough and she had not made relationships that were secure enough for her to feel safe in their hands, especially in her condition. If she lost the baby, they would be the first to put undue pressure on their marriage and having had a taste of Viy, she decided it was wiser to refuse.

She took a gamble that they would be so happy to see a baby they would forget about initiations. They never did, they saw to it that she lived as an outcast for as long as any of them had memory.

Lupapa moved in with the young couple as soon as she received news that the baby was due at any moment. Throughout her stay Mwazi was over the moon at the prospect of being a part in bringing new life into the world. He did not see any dangers, maybe because of Makesa's constant assurance that it would all be okay or knowing that everyone in their lives that could pray was praying for them. Nuns had offered to be informed whether night or day on the moment she went into labour for them to begin prayers for a safe delivery. Culturally labour was considered a form of death and rebirth for the mother. The only person now wondering if she had supported a dangerous decision was Lupapa. From the day she arrived at their home, she was terrified, and it was a daily fight for her to conceal her fear. But the worry found its way in her dreams. Lupapa had not received any confirmation from the ancestors that everything was ok, she felt sure that was a sign she had made a mistake in failing to discourage her daughter from falling pregnant. Upon her arrival she had given Makesa a remedy to make the contractions stronger when the time came, despite the fact doctors had advised her daughter that there was no safe way for her baby to be delivered naturally that would ensure both mother and baby made it to the end of the process with their lives.

Makesa's contractions started at work, but she had heard from women at the village that it was best to wait till they got stronger. She never said it out loud, but deep down her plan was to arrive at the hospital too late for a caesarean. She had been told that having the surgery limited the number of children a woman could have. What would normally have been a sensible balanced woman had been taken over by traditional thinking and faith reliance.

The truth remains that even in a traditional setting she would have been recognised as a high-risk case. The pressures she chose to carry, and the birth plan she wanted were the result of lifetimes of unrelenting and unhealthy expectations on women. Those voices lived in her and had been so entrenched that the dangers of dying during childbirth paled in significance. Who had not heard of new mothers being praised for being strong after having delivered her baby by what was considered natural birth? Especially those that appeared to face labour pain without fear or acknowledged pain, at a time when women died in high number while giving birth. In those days women who expressed their pain were frowned upon. To this day the formal greeting among Makesa's people for a woman, after having delivered a baby to be congratulations for surviving (Mwapusukeni).

As a result, despite new interventions giving a proven record of saving more mothers and babies lives, a latent need for praise due to the woman who faced near death without 'artificial' interventions lingered within the community. Women that had undergone Caesareans shared the news with sadness in their voice. No thought was given to the miracle of both lives having been spared where they might have been lost in the past. Praising women for a good labour may have had a good purpose at one point, but it soon become one more thing to beat women up with as they endured and overcame amazing feats.

When Makesa arrived home from work, she withheld news of her contractions from her mother and husband. She waited until she could no longer ignore the pain, unfortunately for her Mwazi was not home at the time and she was forced to ask her neighbor for help. The lady kindly drove her and Lupapa to the hospital. By the time they arrived the leg Makesa had trouble with was not able to carry her for reasons unknown to her. Her neighbour ran into the hospital and requested a wheelchair on which Makesa was placed and wheeled into the maternity ward. She was in agony, when midwives checked they found that her cervix had dilated to the point it was too far gone for a caesarean. They were all terrified of proceeding because she was a high-risk pregnancy and decided to send for the specialist anyway. Lupapa never made it into the hospital, hearing her daughter cry out that had paralysed her. She knew better, she was a mid-wife, she had lost count of births she had witnessed or heard of where the mother died during delivery from bleeding or general complications, such as a baby not being in the correct position and those incidents where babies had cords tied around their neck. She stood on the hospital lawn convinced that her daughter would join those women. She blamed herself, had she listened to Shikulu and not encouraged her daughter to try for children despite what the doctors told her, she would not be there preparing to lose her child. It all became too much, and she remained on the hospital lawn crying and talking to herself. People walking past her assumed she was one of the patients from the psychiatric ward. She did not care mainly because she could not see them, she was about to die and if life was kind and merciful it would free her from living at the same time it left her daughter's body.

The specialist arrived after what felt like an eternity and upon assessing Makesa announced that it was too late for him to intervene, he told her that they had no way of knowing what childbirth would do to her already injured spine and leg. He expressed frustration that she had waited long before coming in, but Makesa could not hear him, the pain was unbearable and in those moments that was all she could hear. She suddenly felt the urge to push and the nurses realising that they would have to deliver the baby first then deal with mother later, went into auto pilot. The midwife explained to her that it would work better if she listened for them to tell her when to push, they told her that if she worked with them, it would lessen the chances of injuring her private parts and creating other problems or her to contend with to after delivery. Makesa was Shikulu's daughter, one thing she did well was follow instructions, so she listened for their prompts and pushed when they asked her to, only stopping when they told her to do so. This part of the process was not as bad or as painful as the moments before pushing which consisted only of contractions designed to bring terror to any expectant mothers' heart.

Pushing the baby felt less like being tortured and more empowering because on a primal level every physical instinct to release the baby from her body came into play. Her body instinctively knew what the right thing to do was and sent hormones of exhilaration throughout her body, while renewing the strength she felt sure she had lost during contractions. Her brain felt separate to the exercise, it may have been working but in those moment the body was in charge and the only time she felt her brain engage was when voices asked her to "wait" and then to "push".

Mwazi arrived home to find an empty house and after waiting for a short while went to the neighbors to ask if they had seen his wife or mother-in-law. He had never done that before, but something made him worry that day. A young child in the neighbour's house apologised for not listening out for the car and proceeded to recount what had happened. Shock, fear and feelings he could not quite identify came over him, Mwazi forgot he had a car and ran for an hour to the hospital instead. By the time he arrived she was pushing, and he was not allowed in to be with her. Not that he would have asked, men in both tribes never attended the births of their children, the only time the father was present were during unexpected labour otherwise it was not customary for them to attend. The shock of having ran all the way to the hospital hit him and in that moment the honesty of the risk his wife had taken hit him in a way he could no longer deny or pretend he not to see. He knew she wanted children, just as he did, and felt the shame of having put that need before deep reflection on what that meant for her body and her life. As he waited, for new information on his wife and baby's status, it occurred to him that he had not seen his mother-in-law. He asked one of the nursing staff if they had seen her and they informed him that they had no information on their patient coming in with her mother. They were aware of the neighbour who brought her in, but she had left a while ago.

He decided looking for his mother in-law would be a good use of his time while he waited, after searching for a short while, he found Lupapa outside sitting on a lawn talking to herself, looking unwell. Mwazi asked Lupapa to come in and wait with him, but she replied without looking at him that she could not and preferred would wait outside, even in her state she was not ready to verbalise her fears that she was sure daughter would die. He had hoped she would sit with him, as the loneliness and his thoughts were becoming too much for him, however he had no choice but to face all the doubt and fear alone. Mwazi said he would let Lupapa know when he heard anything new. For a moment he wondered if he had said it or thought it because the whole experience felt surreal, he then walked back into the hospital and waited. The nurse came out at some point and informed him that Makesa had delivered a beautiful healthy baby girl. There were concerns about his wife's leg, but the nurse did not share that information with him, they did not even tell Makesa, a decision was made to let her enjoy her early moments with the baby. Mwazi ran out to call Mama, upon hearing that her daughter was still alive, and that both mother and baby were well Lupapa's sense of self and surroundings returned, then she became aware of how terrible she looked. She could not possibly go into the ward and touch her granddaughter in that state; besides she was sure the sight of her would embarrass her daughter, abakashi ba mfumu (the wife of a chief) has to present herself accordingly. As her son-in-law had left his car at home, he searched and managed to find a taxi that could take his mother-in-law home. Lupapa set off to bath and prepare their home for the new arrival. When Mwazi saw his baby daughter, his eyes teared up, and this embarrassed his wife, she was used to singing, drunkenness and loud sounds of joy from new fathers, but tears made her uncomfortable. She did not say anything, but

151

her embarrassment was felt by him, and he promptly wiped his eyes. He picked his baby up and promised her that he would care for her always, that she had a home with his people forever, that he would protect her for as long as he lived because she was the first of all his household's honour.

Understanding that his wife had been through enough he did not share his experience with his mother-in-law and in truth he would not have known what to say. He briefly explained that mama had gone home to get the house ready for her and the baby. Makesa decided it was safe to leave the baby with him and have a shower to clean up after giving birth. To her shock she could not move her legs, Mwazi ran to the nursing staff careful not to be annoying as they had done so much for his wife, had this been at home with his people, there would have been women to help her and explain to him what was happening. He calmly waited for the nurses to finish what they were doing before informing them that his wife told him she could not move her legs. The nurses looked at him as though he was stating the most obvious fact and replied with an accent "of cos she can't, dat iz why we told her she needed C-section", I'll tell one of tha nases to bring her a wheelchair, theez women think they are very clever, now she can't walk. Tha doctor will see her when he is ledi,". She rolled her eyes and walked away, he decided not to tell his wife about the nurse's response, he was terrible at delivering bad news, he especially hated being the bearer of bad news to his wife. Mwazi told her the nurses would be coming over to explain what needed to be done. But she was scared, she remained breastfeeding her baby sitting in a state that felt unclean to her, had she been home with her people she would have been washed by now. Makesa decided to override her strong instinct to bath and focus all her attention on the baby and breast feeding. Later Mwazi was asked to leave and its only then that he discovered that his wife would not be discharged that day.

In the morning the specialist informed her that they needed to carry out further examinations and tests to better understand what was causing her current condition. They advised that the process would be slow, and that she had to allow a week in their care while they put together a plan for what to do about her physical health. Lupapa brought food for her in the days that followed as Makesa preferred not to eat hospital food, her time in hospital meant that the massaging and healthcare Lupapa was there to provide her daughter had to wait, by now Makesa would have been put through the process of inspecting and helping her body recover from having given birth. Most new mothers loved that time as the tenderness and massages given from shoulders, stomach down to the feet were healing and made their bodies feel renewed. The food they ate was designed to assist with healing and stimulation of breast milk production. Lupapa was so thankful that her daughter was alive; she was happy to modify and accommodate all cultural practices around her daughter's hospital stay.

What Lupapa did ask for was to be allowed water to massage the baby every evening as was done for all newborn babies. She brought a clean basin to the hospital, African nurses recognising her Elder position were more than willing to provide all other items she requested. They brought her water in containers at varying temperatures as she requested, each stage of massaging required a specific water temperature. Lupapa would then dip her hands in and transfer that temperature onto baby's body. By the end of the massage and bath the baby would be fast asleep and at peace. There were many benefits to the massage for the baby. There was also a cultural belief that babies that were massaged tended to be more flexible as they got older, considering how they lived, worked, walked, danced, and made love, flexibility was an asset. It was no surprise that many parents wanted that their children to be flexible. Traditional midwives were trained in performing this massage in modified versions should the unexpected occur and baby was left to develop past the stage baby massage was thought to be most beneficial. Midwives had developed a technique to use on later stage babies, especially as the baby was in that position through no fault of their own.

Before the weekend, the doctor went to see Makesa to discuss what they had learned about her inability to walk. He had good news and new information, he explained to Makesa that having looked at the X-ray and the examinations of her body, he felt surgery was more likely to make matters worse for her. He added that the expertise required to attempt the type of surgical intervention needed to help her was not yet available to them. He hoped that sending her home with a wheelchair and crutches for support would help for the time being, he advised Makesa that they planned to observe her body in the coming weeks, which meant she would be required to return for further checks. He assured her that they would continue to search for opportunities to intervene in a way that benefitted her recovery. He believed methods on how to proceed without causing further damage to her bodies would become clearer to them over time.

Makesa went home soon after that discussion, as she was on maternity leave and with Mama there to help her, she took the time to focus on getting physically better and bonding with her baby. She never went back to the doctor and as soon as she was able to walk, she carried on with her life. Makesa had no desire to explore possible interventions, she credited her mind for getting her as far as she had come and decided mental strength along with prayer would get her through any future physical challenges. Over 40 years later when medicine had made several advancements and she was offered an opportunity to undergo a procedure that would drastically change her physical condition. Doctors marveled at her X-ray, because her spine and ball joint sockets were badly deteriorated. Mostly they could not understand how she had carried on moving and working with what must have been excruciating pain. She explained that after a while pain had become a part of her. Upon hearing this, one of the senior doctors recommended that she attend talking therapy after surgery because in a few months, they expected that she would be walking straight and without pain and they wanted her mind to be ready for what that change would mean for her. The doctor hoped it would help Makesa evaluate who she was and how she planned to live in a world not informed by constant pain and pushing through it.

She thanked the doctor, Makesa could see and appreciated that he was coming from a place of care, and though she did not tell him, she had no intention of making use of the talking therapeutic services he had put her up for. She was quite happy to get her physical body fixed and felt confident she could take it from there. In the present her new baby was given the name Mumba, after Makesa's lost brother as it was believed his spirit was reborn through their daughter.

Movement Without Guidance

Headmaster's whose health had deteriorated rapidly after his granddaughter's passing, finally went to sleep one night and never awoke. He never met baby Mumba, but he left the earth knowing his daughter and baby had made it through the delivery process. Shikulu had requested a simple funeral, with little fuss but the sheer volume of people who turned up daily during the week of his mourning period because he had either changed or touched their lives, added to that those for whom his home had been a warm and safe place, meant that his wish could not be fully honoured. People brought food and drink with them, mostly to make sure that his immediate family would not find themselves in the position of needing to extend Shikulu's funeral party hospitality when all their focus was meant to be on grieving.

Funeral singers would write songs specifically for the deceased person, describing what were their important characteristics and what the deceased person meant to the people left behind, this type of singing was established to add to the devastation of those in mourning specifically to induce heartfelt tears. Funeral singers were so effective that their voices could conjure up tears even from those feeling too empty or heartbroken to cry. The singers were not there for celebratory purposes they were essential and their role at funerals had come about out of necessity. In the past, failure to cry was perceived as so unhealthy for the soul of the grieving people that aunties would resort to beating the family member not crying, to aid them along in their grieving process.

Grief in all its unpleasantness and weight was encouraged as a natural process of freeing a person who may otherwise be left to carry it for too long to their detriment. Another important reason crying was encouraged was for the general health of the community and its inhabitants. A bitter person, a traumatised soul, a broken heart, angry or resentful eventually affected the whole community. That is why long discussions to address all emotional matters that came up in day-to-day living were held especially when the issue had the potential to turn septic. Everyone involved in sensitive or upsetting matters was made to talk things through as soon as the problem was identified. This was imposed whether the affected people were willing to discuss the issue or not. No one wanted calamity to fall upon the village as a result of failure to resolve obvious issues that we understood well.

Funeral singers were paid by the immediate family, that was dictated by custom, those not of the immediate family were not permitted to pay for this service. In that way the family contributed to their healing. The singers would sing songs to break everyone's hearts, then stop for a break to allow people to talk, check in on each other, eat, laugh and feel normal, then as that normality began to creep back in, the singers would begin to sing the songs of sorrow, to remind everyone in attendance the point of the gathering. By the time they dispersed many had left the weight of their grief behind. At the point of Shikulu's transition there was no way to grieve in the healthy cultural prescribed way because the new faith and foreign culture had infected everyone. They knew to play act what the new people called 'proper', Mama having been influenced by Shikulu and her own studying of other ways had changed much of her views as well. She broke from convention as she joined in with the cooking for the funeral party. She wanted them to understand she was stoic and reliable. They knew it felt wrong, but times had changed, and they played along because when all was said and done, she had lost half of her and beating her or singing songs of sorrow to force her into accepting the truth of her feelings had been assessed as being of little use to her, so they did not try.

The only time Mama cried in a broken way was when she was drunk. She did not throw herself about in the way past drunken funeral crashers did to conceal the fact they never knew the deceased and were there only to feast and drink. But she was obviously inebriated whenever she cried. People knew things were not right with Lupapa, they knew her responses were not of their way. But they felt they needed to evolve with the times, because that is how they had survived for so long. If pretending to look like they believed Lupapa was coping fine, then that was what they needed to do for her in her moment of grief. They rarely discussed it among themselves, but lately everything felt out of joint, the invaders had somehow escalated the changes in the way people approached and viewed life. They were on a learning fast track that was out of their control. At the funeral their denial of what was plain to see got to the point no one even questioned how much alcohol Mama was consuming, no one attempted to step in as they were all living in mentally exhausting times, with everyone grappling to find their feet.

Mama had second sight which she defined to her granddaughter as the ability to see things that the new people would label as delusion, insanity or plain superstition. But she had two ways of seeing, the one that everyone possessed and then there was another sight that unlocked a part of her allowing her to see what others were planning even before that vibration reached their hearts. The new faith marked this sight as forbidden but denying that it was real did not stop her ability or the fact the future would find its way into her heart and dreams. Shikulu had been her stability, while she tested and investigated the phenomena, his regimented life and trust in the new sciences helped as tools for her to discover what type of sight it was and what evidence she could put together to reach a conclusion as to whether it was simple delusion or something else. As Shikulu got more and more unwell that aspect of her had begun to be grow uncontrollably. She could see people's plans for her, and others close to her. She found herself learning what was in the now and what was in the yet to come. When Shikulu died the door to her second sight that she had spent years tugging at gingerly, flew opened forcefully and the remaining knowledge flowed into her without restraint.

At the latter part of Shikulu's funeral there was a celebration, and everyone took comfort in knowing that his soul and mind had transitioned to a space where his physical body could no longer be a hinderance to his abilities. Mitondo was sure that his departure was their gain. Before everyone left, Makesa having reflected on the fact that Kunda had taken in their brother's sons, declared without speaking to her husband that any of her siblings who needed to step into the future could also move in with her and her husband. Everyone at the funeral thought this was a good idea, praised her and went back to their normal days and routines as they were sure it was what Shikulu would have wanted.

When Mwazi's family caught wind of this revelation, his sisters specifically Viyoletti, decided they wanted their children to live with their brother and be a part of the plan they had all heard so much about. One of the children they decided needed to move in without discussion was young Peter, Mwazi's nephew from one of his siblings. Makesa was happy to have him and at that point their home had six dependents including baby Mumba. Mwazi and Makesa were using every resource and contact they had to help the young people in their care, they did not want to admit it, but they were drowning. The stress was immense, a big part of their budget was going to supporting the dependents in their household and it soon became necessary to employ people who could help cook and clean as well. Life became unbearably stressful for the young couple.

Mwazi's people were making noise about the number of people from Makesa's family in their brother's home. His people had no intention of being left behind. Makesa upon observing the slow trickle of extra bodies into their home from her husband's family, wrote and asked her mother for counsel. Lupapa advised her daughter to keep having children of her own, she believed it would put a stop to others freeing themselves of their responsibilities by leaving their children in Makesa's care. She added that in her experience an empty home encouraged such behaviour. Lupapa emphasised that the vision we carried was for our people because only our people had the discipline to execute the work that needed to get done. Having no ideas of her own to address her problems, Makesa decided to continue risking her life and physical health, further with every pregnancy that followed. It was just after she delivered her third child when disaster hit. Eneri and Kunda's neighbors had written to Mitondo. They were from Mitondo and had witnessed shocking abuse. They told stories of two young boys being left to sleep outside, the neighbour's own children recounted horrific tales of the treatment that they had seen the young boys endure. It included being denied food and stories of horrific beatings and neglect. They had heard screams from the beatings and had also seen scars on the young boy's bodies, the children were clearly terrified of the lady of the house and her husband was rarely home. They had initially asked their children not to play with the traumatised boys because the stories the parents heard were chilling and evil, and they did not want their children witnessing such horror so early in their lives. But also, because city life was draining and did not allow room for the hands-on community spirit, they were accustomed to giving and receiving at home.

Luckily restlessness in their souls would not allow them to ignore the abuse any longer, plus at the core of them lay a strong instinct to help the children. The adults struggled to name the horrors they had heard to relatives because for them there were no words for what Eneri was doing to the boys. They also added that they were sure that the little they knew was nowhere close to the whole story. The neighbours decided from that point on to put their collective energy into finding out whose people their neighbors came from, so that they could ask them to intervene to put a stop to the abuse. It was fortunate that they found Kunda's people first had they found Eneri's instead, the children would be dead.

Lupapa upon hearing that her first born's children were being abused in ways that she had lived her whole life never having witnessed enraged her. People sent to investigate from Mitondo confirmed the truth of the allegations and struggled to share all the information in its entirety. Eneri was sick, she was dangerous and because her type of sickness was unfamiliar, they struggled to put together an appropriate solution aside from taking the boys home to Mitondo with them immediately. When word got round to Makesa about how Mumba's children were being treated, her response was to drive to Kunda's prestigious office and when she found him proceeded to physically assault him to the point security had to step in. Kunda did not fight, he did not argue, he knew his home was a mini version of hell on earth. Kunda's marriage had deteriorated in part because his home was so bad that he had found a second wife and was living with her rather than with Eneri and their sons. Both Kunda and Eneri's children had been diagnosed with mental illnesses that affected their development, the first child had managed to slip past their watchful eye initially, but they soon find out he was also very unwell and would prove to be, not only incredibly intelligent but unable to function well in society, many women and men suffered at his depraved hands. Up until his death everyone asked Kunda why he never took his brother's children along with him when he moved to his second wife's home? He never had an answer for them.

For those not aware of his homelife, Kunda was a dignified married man, in reality his wife frightened him, it did not stop him from having intimate moments with her that eventually resulted in nine children in total, maybe he did that in the hope one of the children would be well. But there was no hiding that Eneri was too unhinged for him to live with full-time. Their home was not unlike a prison, she had locks made for all the doors in the house and shockingly for their culture, she had keys made for the pantry and the fridge as well. This behavior was unheard off as food in Mitondo was always made available to all, locking it away was a strange concept. Another reason Eneri's behavior was unsettling was, the two of them were incredibly wealthy, no one could understand why she felt the need to lock food away. Kunda's home was described by the few people that still made the effort to visit them as a cold place. The joy his people were accustomed to feeling within a family was absent in his home.

Even with her rage Makesa did not direct it at Eneri. She knew the woman was unwell, and no one wanted to touch her, physically or otherwise also Makesa was also bound by cultural conduct, all her grievances had to be directed to the person in the marriage to whom she was related. Her anger was rightly directed at her brother because he took those boys willingly and she planned to hold him to his commitment.

Rage was not all Makesa felt with the situation, she felt helpless. She would happily have taken both boys into her home, but she also had a problem at home that made her desire to move the boys in near impossible. Viy's Mozambique dream had not come to fruition. Dingi was struggling to afford a house that could accommodate his new wife and four children. Somehow being away from her beauty and warmth woke him up to the reality that an instant family was something of a challenge. Viy who was still besotted had no plans of giving up on Dingi, she packed her bags and left her people without warning and headed to Mwazi's home, she arrived a day later with four children in tow. Viy then declared that if her brother was doing well enough to take in Makesa's siblings, he was wealthy enough to take in her children, freeing her to start a new life with her husband.

Mwazi refused without hesitation, he knew that unlike the adults from Makesa's family, Viy's children were young and needed intensive hands-on care. Viy's children's needs whether emotional, physical, spiritual, or cultural would add a new level of stress on his marriage. Mwazi knew it would be too much for them especially as they were still very much a new couple even though culturally, they were considered closer to being Elders. They had not been given enough time to establish a secure financial foundation. Viy was incensed when he declined to take her children and of course she blamed Makesa. This was also strategic as Viy knew that the person to add pressure to in order to achieve her desired outcome was her brother's wife. Where Makesa's family's rules of engagement with in-laws was to speak to your spouse and ask them to intervene. Viy had every intention of taking this fight directly to her sister-in-law, who she believed had interrupted a well-oiled ecosystem that had benefitted her lifestyle very well in the past. She decided time had come for Makesa to leave and especially as at this point Makesa she was expecting their third child it would mean less resources from her brother to her. Viy decided the friend she had planned for her brother was much more malleable and less likely to cause her problems. She also rationalised that with only two children at that point, extracting Makesa from the family and replacing her with the more suitable friend would cause less discord with her parents. Makesa had seen the game being played by Viy, she was already living under immense stress before Viy arrived. A house full of people with varying needs had been taking its toll on her.

The young couple paid for all their dependent's educational and general needs. Stress was a state of being that Makesa had been trying her best to avoid. Pregnancy was a responsibility she took seriously and everything she knew told her an unhappy expecting mother was bad for the baby. Making a pregnant woman cry or sad was forbidden in Mitondo, but she was now among people who lived by different rules so the safety she would have been afforded as a result of her condition was not available in her third pregnancy. Every day in her home was war, because Viy saw to that. She knew nothing killed a new marriage quicker than constant strife and she planned to lean on them at every given opportunity.

They had also received word that Fiela was on hunger strike until Mwazi took his sister's children in. The only reason this matter had not escalated further as a result of his mother's action was because Shikulu Nzendo did not approve of what his daughter was doing. Whilst he found Viy's bad behavior amusing, an able mother fighting to unburden herself of children, leaving her free to run off with a lover was not something he felt he could support. That is not to say he stepped in to discourage the bad behavior either. But his silence diminished much of the power the threats directed at Makesa and Mwazi might have had otherwise carried.

Mwazi was conflicted, he loved his mother as far as he could remember he had done everything that he could to be at her side and supportive. But he had a wife now and an important saying had been shared with him just before his marriage by an Elder. His uncle called him and asked him a question, he said if you were lost and walked up to a person with mouths all around their head and all the mouths were speaking at the same time, which one would you listen to? Mwazi thought about it a bit but in the end, he admitted that he did not know. His uncle replied you listen to the mouth directly under your nose. That mouth symbolises your wife, if you are sure that you are making a wise decision in marrying the woman you claim to love then, when the world comes to you and they are all speaking and demanding your attention especially in difficult times, your wife is the voice that you listen to. His uncle added that though family helped with choosing wives, they always based their decision on the woman who was the best fit for the man so that listening to her counsel felt like a natural thing to do.

When news of Kunda's horrific neglect of their brother's children was brought to her, it all became too much for Makesa to handle. Fighting him was dangerous in her condition, but the relentless storm she had been living under because of Viy's behaviour, meant that every decision Makesa made had to be with the understanding that all she loved was already at stake. She only drove to Kunda's office when it became apparent to her that she was out of ideas on what was a useful solution to her problems. She beat him to make him do the right thing. She punched him because he had failed their brother, she kept hitting because she was in hell, because her moments of marital bliss felt unfairly short lived, and he took the assault because he was also living in hell.

Kunda never laid a hand on her, he hated that he had failed his brother, being assaulted felt like something he deserved. He had no parenting skills to speak off. Kunda's abilities lay in being able to plan and mobilise workers to fight, he was a hunter and excelled in all the things that had been encouraged in him as a young person. He convinced himself that leaving the boys with a monster was easier than trying to parent them himself. Kunda also feared that his own children with her were not safe, but he had a place in his brain where he stored that worry and those thoughts rarely resurfaced to unsettle him. In the end, all nine children Eneri conceived with Kunda were diagnosed with varying mental health issues that affected their ability to function well in society. If Kunda could not protect his own children how could anyone expect him to protect his brother's children? It was easier to take a beating for failing, then he could go home to his new wife and forget his other hellish existence. Time spent with his second wife was joyful and tranquil, it had also produced two daughters who were lovely; with his second wife Kunda had the family he had always wanted. He did not share his inner thoughts with Makesa as she pummeled him, instead he promised to do better and protect the boys. But as soon as the workday was complete, and he carried on as before.

Their people spoke to Makesa, and recounted the horrors they had witnessed, the Elders wasted no time in informing Kunda and Makesa that they had both failed their brother and added that it would have been better to take the boys back to the safety of the community, than to leave them in the city under the guise of exposing them to a better life, only for them to be abused and neglected. The siblings could only reiterate that, they believed living with them in the city is what their brother would have wanted for his children. They spoke quickly and with passion as losing the boys would be a failure, they felt they could never recover from. Kunda and Makesa were reminded that other children left behind by parents who had moved to cities in search of employment, were living better lives than the two boys.

When Kunda was questioned over what was going on in his home, he did not deny what had been recounted. He was hardly home because he could not bear being around his wife, and he said as much in the meeting. Kunda explained that he wanted a loving home and that is what he had with his second wife. At the time the meeting was being held, Eneri had been making the two boys sleep outside with the dogs and chickens. The children told stories of being starved and Eneri's rule to have a lock on every food door. She applied this rule even with the cook and cleaners, they were never allowed to hold the keys, to the pantry, fridge, or the freezer, waiting for madam as they called her to hand them the daily portioning of food as she preferred to do.

Kunda being an avid hunter, would go on hunting trips where he would return with tonnes of bush meat, which Eneri would lock away. Prior to their marriage Kunda shared the game from his hunts with friends and family, but Eneri put a stop to that. The meat would rot as a result, then she would go to the extent of disposing of the meat at a location far from her home, such was her commitment to depriving anyone in her home from benefitting from her gain even when it involved spoiled food.

Between the beatings, starvation and general torture, most that heard what happened in Kunda's home refused to accept the story entirely, when they held discussions among themselves, they would take care to add that it was important to consider that perhaps the children may have exaggerated because the truth was too disturbing for them to accept. But however much the adults struggled with the truth, what the children were saying was true. The clothes they had on were unwashed and covered in visible blood stains, yet people preferred to be selective in what they believed, adding that what they had accepted was bad enough.

Makesa begged her people for another chance, and when she was asked how doing so was not as good as signing the boy's death sentence? Even in her desperation, Makesa had decided against sharing her experience with Eneri. She knew full well they would ask her why knowing what Eneri did, had she allowed children in that home with saying a word? The truth was she had never imagined Eneri would harm children, Makesa had assumed the vitriolic treatment she had experienced was as a result of being a grown up and they were newlyweds at that time. Makesa was also aware that they were expected to share information, which is one of the safety measures that they lived by, also because information sharing created an opportunity for everyone to grow, in all the forms growth manifested. As she did not have what she felt were satisfactory answers to the questions they would ask her, it was simpler to fight for a second chance without dredging up her hidden ugly experience.

Kunda stepped in as she pleaded and suggested that perhaps only having one child in his care would help matters, his idea was that the older of the two boys also called Mumba remain with him, that would ensure that the boy could go to work with him when he was not at school and join his uncle during the hours he was not at home. Kunda promised that his nephew would never leave his side for any reason. However, he was informed that Mumba was the child they feared for the most, and if he was not removed from that environment, they expected to receive news of his death. His younger brother Kunda on the other hand appeared stronger, even after what had been done to them. Of the two boys Kunda was seen as being in a better position to remain with his uncle. Makesa took this a chance to redeem them both and offered to take Mumba on the understanding that her brother would protect his young brother as he had promised to do among witnesses. The Elders found this plan acceptable.

When all was said and done, Kunda failed to keep his promise to protect his nephew, it was not long before he started leaving young Kunda alone with his abusive wife and being conscious of the meeting that had transpired Eneri had modified her torture methods. Many wondered how a woman who ran several businesses found the time to be sadistic to a young child, what was worse was she never hid or denied her abuse. It was almost as though she felt her actions were normal behaviour. Kunda had never shared this with anyone, but her thinking and emotional detachment to disturbing acts she executed scared him, he also never shared how she once smashed a bottle on his head because he had come home late one night. What Kunda found alarming was her face remained unchanged throughout. No anger though she did smile oddly, Eneri always smiled inappropriately.

The Elders were right, young Kunda was strong, he found a way to navigate living in what was a torture asylum, the plan hatched by his uncle was not sound in the first place as taking a young person regularly to an environment like his workplace was not feasible, to begin with there were several safety issues he had not considered. Young Kunda never forgot that a decision had been made to leave him alone in hell, he never forgave the adults that failed to see his innocence and vulnerability. He resented the decision made to save his brother as it felt to him that his own young life was valued as less than his brother's. Kunda created a wall around him that no one would ever be able to penetrate and touch him. He lived in hell until his late teens. He learned to keep Eneri happy and off his back and over time this seemed to work. Her sons grew more terrifying as they got older, in part because their mental health deteriorated, and their parent's refusal to accept that they needed medical intervention. The environment the boys lived in exacerbated their violent impulses.

This meant that a decent night's sleep was not always an option for young Kunda. He learned to put a barrier at his door to keep him safe, he barricaded his door every night. His father's people had failed him, he watched as his brother healed and began to thrive. Where he struggled in school due to abuse, his brother was now excelling. Knowing that his father took to running off to his second wife again only made his anger burn. University literally saved his life because after that he never returned to the house of horror.

Meanwhile back at Makesa's house just as she had returned with one of her nephews in tow. Viy woke up one morning having made travel arrangements and the important decision to leave her four children with her mother at Mwazi's house with instructions that he fulfil his duty to her or refuse and force his elderly mother to care for her children. Either way she would leave. Viy had taken this action because the day before, the couple's family priest had come to visit, and this was no coincidence, word had gone round about what was happening to the young couple. The priest confirmed the story with Makesa, as Mwazi had told him everything was okay. His wife saw an opportunity to get someone who was not family to intervene. She also secretly hoped that racism would work in her favor, and maybe this would be the one person Viy would not tear apart because of the new poison indoctrinated by the invaders. She was wrong if anything Makesa cringed as she watched her arrogant sister-in-law look down her nose at someone, they all called a holy man. He was adamant that she leave their home and take her children with her. He added that the fact that theirs were the first nuptials he had conducted, he was not willing to stand by and allow anyone to tear them apart. After he had spoken including advising her to ask the fathers of the children to care for them. Earlier she had indicated to him that she did not understand English. She did but refused to speak it. Fr Jude had asked Mwazi to translate, Mwazi knew Viy understood the language, but translated anyway knowing full well his sister could hear exactly what the priest was saying. Viy stood up when she had heard enough, she stared at him long enough to let him know he was no authority to her and walked out of the lounge. Everyone was shocked at the disrespect even her brother who felt the priest had been measured and reasonable. Viy leaving first thing in the morning without her children was her response to that meeting.

Mwazi was relieved when he found she had left. His relationship with his mother had always been a close one and with his sister gone, his mother was more likely to hear him. He first asked her to please make time for him and spoke to her in humility. She loved him and the fact Viy was gone meant Fiela no longer felt pressure to look angry all the time. He explained again why the children could not stay, in the same way he had before, but this time he promised her that any children or grandchildren of hers who needed to complete their education but were without means, he would provide for them without question. He asked that she please allow them to stabilise their home and their finances and then they could comfortably bring others along with them when they were more secure. Fiela accepted this arrangement because she believed that Mwazi would do what he said and finally there was peace in his home.

Eneri hated Lupapa and this was well known in the family, the truth was she was terrified of her. Her mother-in-law was the only person that made her squirm and reduce her to childlike disposition, behind her back Eneri called Lupapa a witch, not in the traditional sense but in the way the invaders labelled women 'witch'. The stigma attached to that word for our people was significant. Lupapa did not care when she was told. She wanted Eneri to fear her. Everyone had heard what Lupapa, who by now was elderly woman had done to the man who tried to burgle her home. He believed an elderly woman alone would be easy pickings. When she apprehended him, Lupapa decided to send a message to anyone who thought they could do the same. She used her hunting knives to slice his testicles off and left them on display at her front door. She heard the man had lived after what she had done, but her point had been made. Lupapa could use a rifle comfortably, she was skilled in art of using a knife to skin an animal and defend herself. But Eneri was right there was something else about her that no one had been able to give a name to. Eneri was the only one to name it, but she chose that word out of fear.

People generally found themselves hesitating before attempting to engage Lupapa especially as she grew older, many that knew her approached with reverence because of her long record of service to the people and there was that other thing about her they could not quite put their finger on. No one ever said out loud how special she was in a way that was not of this world to her face. As Lupapa was loved by her community and when Eneri called her witch, it only confirmed everyone's belief that Eneri was an unstable woman. Despite it being against their traditional rules of engagement with in-laws, Lupapa on a visit to the see her children had threatened to kill Eneri after what she had to the children, Eneri believed she could do it. She was right Lupapa was angry that she had been bound from killing the woman by her people, but it did not stop her from waiting for Eneri to give her the opportunity to end her. Eneri never touched the boy in the same way from that point on. But by then it was too late the scars in him externally and internally had become set. As everyone was trying to find their feet in the new world, it meant there was less time and opportunity to tend to young Kunda's healing. His anger protected him from the pain he felt at losing his father, then losing his mother who was too poorly to care for him, followed by what felt like a lifetime of abuse and rejection. All he had was his anger which also gave him strength. Deep down he knew that his real spirit would not have been able to survive in the world he inhabited, anger had become a survival tool.

During his time at university, home for young Kunda alternated between living with friends and church members, until he found a job that could help him pay for a small flat. His father never noticed any of this because he was never home and Makesa remained none the wiser, leaving young Kunda a living breathing ticking bomb within their family. When Makesa's third baby was born she did not take maternity leave. She could not, too many people depended on her and the weight of the double standards which were really racist attitudes at work had started to feel heavy. A home with three young children and a houseful of dependents pushed her stress to peak levels. She had hired a young lady who claimed to be from a village near Mitondo. She was traditionally respectful and organised. She had been sent to the city for the purpose of making money to support her mother back home, it helped that when they met her, she expressed a love for children and added that having been told all about Makesa's wonderful home she wanted nothing more than to help look after Makesa's children just as she would her own children someday. Makesa was happy with her, this decision may have come from a place of desperation, but the young lady was very charming, and Makesa hired her without further thought.

Months passed and she felt secure that her children were in capable hands, which is why she was surprised to receive a phone call at work from Joy, informing her that she had come home from college to find the newborn had had an accident and her head and lips were swollen, her injuries were bad enough that adults who saw her believed the baby needed to be taken into hospital immediately. After the call Makesa went to her manager's office and explained what had happened to her baby, the first thing he asked her was why the child minder could not take the baby to the hospital as he saw no need to approve a request for what was a personal matter that could be addressed outside work hours. Makesa was mortified, in all the years she had worked for the bank she had watched both white men and women request days off for the most ridiculous reasons. There was one woman they all had to cover because despite doing as little as was humanly possible, she refused to work during her monthly cycle due to feeling unwell. As for the white men, their absence was their business and if they shared a reason for being absent at all it was because to them something dramatic had happened. The Africans were aware that every inane reason a white person gave for absence at work did not translate into an opportunity for them to do the same. But her daughter in need of medical attention, her sibling who was part of her support system had felt it necessary to call her which meant the incident was critical. The manager maintained that Makesa make other arrangements for her child to be taken to the hospital. For the first time Makesa refused to bite her tongue and said "Mr Smith I have worked here for years never taken holidays or sick days off. My maternity leave has never been longer than a month, yet now when I have an emergency and have to be there for my child, you deny my request". He refused to budge. She considered beating him up but chose to walk out of his office and the building never to return.

When she arrived home, she found her baby still bleeding, her mouth swollen her head double in size and immediately rushed her to the hospital. The hospital was concerned and advised her that the baby needed to be admitted into hospital for further checks. Joy told Makesa that when she got home from school, she found the child minder and an unknown person chatting while the baby slept in the baby basket covered in blood. When she asked them what happened, they laughed and nonchalantly recalled how she fell but did not offer any details. When Joy asked them why, when it happened, they had not called Makesa immediately? The young ladies did not even concern themselves with responding to the question.

Prior to working for Makesa, their childminder had been told of the new opportunity in the cities to help desperate mothers in need of childcare. Such was the desperation and demand that childminders meant they held demigod status at that point. Most working parents did not want to argue with childminders because that meant interfering with their own jobs which was their source of income, making parents slaves to imperialists, employers and childminders. Her baby falling badly was also the childminder's first test of whether the parents would dare lose their precious jobs to challenge her handling of the situation.

Either way she did not care the city was full of desperate families that needed bending into submission. When Joy came home and enquired about the baby with a swollen head, the childminder maintained a defiant demeanor that dared Joy to push her further. She felt secure the lady of the house's sister would not want the responsibility of being the reason the parents lost the child's helper entirely. In the early days of childminding, she had seen to it that she made herself indispensable to them as a household. Though she was not required to, she did the cooking, cleaning, and all other household chores, this was all part of her human training, she planned to become like a drug for them. No one ever thought to stop her from doing all jobs unrelated to hers, nor did they ask her how she provided the baby all the necessary attention if she was tending to so many other tasks at the same time. They enjoyed what felt like her positive and helpful contributions in the home and that was her plan. This game plan occurred to Makesa while at the hospital as doctors informed her that her baby's jaw had been inexplicably dislocated. She knew that she had been played and she wanted to kill the young lady, but her children needed her, and feeling helpless she cried. The legal system being what it was, she felt there was no point in putting her family through the pain of a process which would mostly cost her money and she suspected would only produce a judgment more likely leave them all feeling empty. But for her faith, her father's vision, Mwazi and all the children that needed her, she would have seriously entertained following through with killing the childminder. Instead, she instructed Joy to tell the childminder to leave immediately, because if she ever set eyes on her again, Makesa planned to end her. Years later she regretted giving this warning and wished she had followed through with her initial instinct to permanently erase the lying reckless creature.

Starting Over

Makesa never returned to the bank. When they rang her, a day later enquiring as to her whereabouts in a stern voice. She wasted no time informing them that the fact they placed greater value on a colleague's period pain days off, over her child's hospital emergency, meant she had no interest in working for them. She gave them a further mouthful about how she had foolishly assumed working in excellence counted for anything at their bank. She concluded by saying she would rather be unemployed with less money, than work for them under those conditions, especially at a time when Black people were supposed to be free from oppression. They did not care and neither did Makesa feel heartbroken at their lack of concern. If anything, staying would have been soul destroying for her.

Mwazi waited until she was receptive to share with her the security and greater presence of our people in every position that could be enjoyed in the civil service. Knowing his wife, he focused his sales pitch on job security, and she agreed to have a look at civil service jobs. He told her that he knew of people that could help them. But she wanted to take time to find the place that would be the right fit for her. For the months that followed, she enjoyed being mother and only that during the day. It was something she often felt conflicted about, as she was always so busy working added to that all the church activities, they were a part off, as well as trying to remain true to as much of her father's vision though her siblings.

After the traumatic episode the family shared the information obtained from the incident concerning childminders in the city with others. By now they understood that this was one of the many uncomfortable realities of city life. The sense of human disconnect, was something they had no language for. In essence they were experiencing the life of a banished person without the stigma. They clung desperately to their stories, songs and culture, but even that felt more like something new rather than continuity.

Their memories of who they were had become a fragmented, it felt forced rather than natural in this new world. It was a daily enough struggle for them to remember that they were human as it was.   Laughing at the invader's warped and poisoned thinking, had been effective for a while but by this point it had begun to lose its power, ignoring them was no longer an option the new arrivals had caused a form of sepsis on the land.

Many in the family were too afraid to say out loud that the mental freedom and that was required by all of them might not be enough to compete with the daily imported toxicity they were forced to fight against.   Those that remembered Headmaster's fears after he returned from the war also remembered his warning and the urgency with which he insisted they prepare well if they had any hope of freeing themselves. For many the reality that it may have been too late to save their identities was hitting home. Self-doubt, self-hate, confusion but worse for the first time in their memory at least, their skin that was like a miracle and had been celebrated as illuminating the land, as it glistened in the sun, the skin that was a backdrop for a smile that could make the pulse race, while lifting the soul. Beautiful Black skin that complemented bright eyes, making them easier to read the inner workings of a person's soul. In this new warfare that beautiful skin had now being labelled opposite to what they had known for all their lives.

They were living in a reality designed to turn them and others into no more than empty shells. Most were exhausted, but there were those among them who desired the shiny new toys that came with the oppressors. Many born after their culture had been began its decline found it easier to assimilate to the new ideas of living. They chose not to question when Bwana (Boss) and Madam struggled with the simplest of tasks, at this point in history everyone even the warriors were tired. It was no longer funny that Madam left others to wash her period-stained clothes and underwear or that she failed to cope with daily life. Nor was Bwana impregnating young Black girls and paying them amusing. Young girls were now being trained to avoid Bwana, but even then, Bwana refused to leave them alone. They accepted that Bwana and Madam felt free to invade their personal spaces, they learned to hide their contempt for these uncultured creatures because they were tired. Young girls knew that Bwana was dishonorable and would deny all knowledge of them and their children when they fell pregnant, and Madam needed to be constantly uplifted even when it was obvious to all that Madam appeared unfit to be living anywhere on earth.

City life was soul destroying with monetary currency as the illusion of reward for what was taken from the workers. Even the invaders looked hollow in the places were life lived, funny enough our people only saw this spiritual death when they had moved to the cities and only after having fully immersed themselves into the new life. Yet even as they witnessed themselves losing their souls, they would never have imagined or believed that in less than fifty years from that point their grandchildren and beyond would consider speaking their language and their customs as secondary or inferior to that of other lands. The ancestors would never have believed this reality, we learn from others, but never lose ourselves in them. Yet that's exactly what would happen to many. They had welcomed them as they had done others before them, learning for the purposes of our survival and even when words like 'protectorate' were banded around by them, to minimize the true extent of the damage caused, the people still hurt and continued to lose.

After walking out of her bank job, Makesa's research led her to an entry point into the civil service that would require retraining, she was looking into the secretarial field. The jobs were well paid, but secretaries that worked for the courts were paid far better than most in the civil service. She came to the conclusion that she needed to study shorthand, if she was serious about getting a job working in the nation's courts. The only college that gave shorthand training was located out of the city and the course was a yearlong without any breaks. She spoke to Mwazi about what was required to obtain the certification she needed. She knew he would be supportive; they shared similar visions for the future, but she was worried about the children who were still very young. Mwazi promised her that between him and the other family members in the house the children would be loved and cared for. He emphasised that it was important for everyone, that she make personal advancement.

Once it was agreed, they made the payment, and from that point there was no turning back. When the departure date was upon them, Mwazi drove his wife to the coach depot at 4 am and it was still dark, they understood that in situations concerning the future of their people, sentimentality took a back seat, this included thoughts of missing your partner, wishing she did not have to go, or expressing the desire not have a duty driving her to other places without him. In that sense they were perfect for each other because they both accepted that the requirement to contribute to future generations was greater than both of them. Makesa's journey to self-improvement at the secluded college ran by Franciscan Nuns begun when she arrived by coach. She discovered quickly that living conditions were basic to bare. There were more women who were younger in age than she was. In fact, Makesa was one of the few women her age who were also married with a family taking the course.

The first day of class, Sister Margareta, looked at all the late twenty something year old students and declared loudly "I do not plan to spend too much time on you, at your age grasping shorthand will be difficult. In my experience many of you will drop out, the family baggage most of you now carry is too heavy for you to master a new skill and you'll lack the focus to pick up the intricacies of shorthand properly". Makesa had experience in various learning environments, but this was the first time she had heard an educator speak to students in that way. Even nursing, or what she could remember of it was not as bad as what she had just heard. There was a competitive edge in nursing of course and most young ladies had plans to graduate with an aim to use the degree as currency to secure a suitable husband. Many of the nurses she met in training had no intention of getting their hands dirty. Makesa was furious that while this college been more than happy to take all their money, they knew full well their focus would be limited to the younger ladies while the rest were relegated to being unteachable before they had even begun. What they had never counted on was that Makesa was her father's daughter in every way.

The introduction by the first Nun was only a taste of what would follow. It was clear to every student that the Nuns had no business teaching anyone, they labelled any lack of understanding as the fault of the student not a requirement to adjust the teaching method. Upon discovering this Makesa decided that she would have to take ownership of her own learning and use the studying methodology she knew as the tool to her advancement. The library became her home after class. Makesa discovered that the Nuns were right about something, for some reason the older students were slower to grasp the concept of shorthand. It did not help that the younger students were not only encouraged more by the teaching staff, but they were also given more support. Makesa did not indulge in despair at the unfairness knowing that it would do her no good. She resolved to using the classroom as foundation learning and then she would have to do the rest of the work and practise required by herself. Soon enough Makesa was the fastest shorthand writer in her class, she was not distracted by the shock or acknowledgment, her goal was to achieve such high grades that when she left school there would be no job that would deny her achievement on paper.

Then distractions that momentarily tugged at her heart started to invade her tunnel vision. This intrusion came from her peers who were wives and mothers themselves, which was the only reason Makesa entertained them slightly more than the others. After class, Makesa found Matilda crying, word had gone round the college that her husband had moved another woman into their home. People had seen him with the new woman enough times to be concerned, some had even seen the woman around Matilda's children. That news sidetracked Matilda's learning, and completely knocked her focus on study. The affair, the sightings with another woman, she could understand, but her husband exposing their children to her was something she could not ignore or forgive. After that, sleep became impossible for Matilda. Accepting her husband's need for female company was never her problem. Replacing her as mother with another woman as an unacceptable betrayal.

Because Makesa could not ignore the ruckus building up around her, she thought she could help by advising Matilda to do what she had done, that was to inform her family or friends not to write or update her on any family news unless it was absolutely necessary because she believed that imagery or stories of her family would make any mother want to return home, and that was not an option for her. But Matilda being a free agent insisted on writing and requesting further details, her distress at the news that followed began to affect not only Makesa's psych but the other students as well. Even Makesa began to wonder if her Mwazi was getting tired of living with all the family and no intimate companion beside him, that wonder turned to worry. Some wives had started writing and asking neighbors or family to check on their husbands. A shocking number were heartbroken, others could not get confirmation which felt worse than knowing.

Their fears and worry started to get to Makesa's head, and her focus became divided, then one day the truth found her. As much as Mwazi was her love, as much as he was the only man, she knew she would ever love, the only person who looked at her as whole, the one who saw only beauty despite her visible limp. His good heart, his supportive character, his love, and yes, his warm skin every time she needed it. The truth of the matter was Mwazi was just a man in a story bigger than all of them and if he felt that time had come to leave her, then that is what he would do. She had training to complete because the one thing she would never forget was the vision her father stored in all his children. She never wrote home, she separated herself from all the students and their stories of pain. She even closed herself off from those with joyful news choosing to focus only on her reasons for being on the course. Makesa wanted to be able to return home knowing that she had completed what she had set out to do.

Makesa was not heartless to the point of failing to say goodbye to those women who could no longer remain in college, even some young ones left. Makesa's goodbyes were polite, some cultural and mostly always in recognition of the humanity of all those young ladies and women. What those departures never became was an opportunity to derail the journey she was on. Pretty soon all the students understood that about her.

Makesa was the perfect model student, eventually they started to emulate her behavior to be able to reach her high standard of work and achievement. The other students followed her routine and woke up in the early hours of the night to practice their drilling, the same as she did. Shikulu would have been proud, what Makesa's shorthand peers would never know is that of all her father's young future visionaries, she was not the best. But she made sure to impact every environment she occupied; this was also testament to Shikulu's training. The young people that went to his school made sure that when they went out into the world, they were hard to miss.

No Nun ever admitted to being wrong in those days, the best you could hope for was their delayed praise, and by then Makesa did not need it. However, she was smart enough to know not to upset them by correcting their self-congratulatory attitude to her excellence and success. She also saw no benefit in drawing negative attention to herself by being labelled as ungrateful. She allowed them to feel and present to everyone that she was a product of nothing but their hard work and good teaching. For the most part all they ever did was reinforce the unequal environment; the country was still operating under. The experience at the college did trigger Makesa's eagerness to prove an abuser wrong just as the younger version of herself had been conditioned to do by an abusive Eneri. The time her last days at the college came about, every Scholar/ educator at the college would point to her as the student to aspire to become. Makesa being Shikulu's child never allowed any of that noise to interfere with her focus or her target grade. She knew that more than anything that she needed what they called a First-class grade, that result alone would give her the edge required to continue her journey and get the job she wanted with greater ease. By the time she had completed her final exams everyone at the college was convinced that only injustice, injury or a total mental block could stand in the way of Makesa achieving a First in her results.

The day of the final exam for Makesa was like any other day of practice for her, she treated every school day, every test, every moment as though it was her last. Her final exam came with all the pressure that she felt daily, this was a state of being that she was now accustomed to. When the shorthand exam was done, and she had completed her course, she left without any doubt in her mind that she had given the very best that she had to give, and now it was time to return home.

The exams were marked abroad, everyone had to wait for their results for over a month.

Makesa returned home at the end of term, feeling confident that her results would be good. This thought also came with acceptance that, it was too late to do anything to change her results now and time had come to focus on home and its needs. Makesa was happy to see her children, though the youngest of them did not recognise her, and cried when Makesa ran to hug her. She never said it at the time, but it broke her heart. She remained home while waiting for her results, Makesa used her waiting time to plan the ways to give her the opportunity that she would need to get a good job when she received her results. She used the time at home to gather information on people holding senior positions in civil service areas, then she broadened that to all people in power positions at the offices she had selected as ideal for her. Mwazi and many of her college peers may have been doing well but most were not well connected, and competition was fierce. Their society being what it was then, one either knew someone in a position of power or had family members with connections, failing that there was always good old-fashioned bribing. Makesa did not have the money or societal standing, to bribe those in senior or powerful positions and they would never have considered taking money from just anyone, there were rules of engagement involved in bribing.

Little, lower, less than, insignificant whatever pejorative you could imagine for people not considered of the upper class, applied now in their society and everyone knew their place enough to never offer bribes to those in the higher tiers or as they were called locally the upper mwambas. A new class system had entered our consciousness, dynasties reliant on names were being established. It was not just the job you had, but your name could also open doors. One highly successful person, in most cases translated into all attached family members, including nieces and nephews changing their names from their current surname to that of the now successful relative. This behaviour was new for them, aside from being a descendant in the line of the chieftain or royalty it was mostly accepted that we were all human first, living for community and family. The new way changed all of that, being highly educated or one life changing business deal elevated people, in what appeared to be a random system. At first that system was attractive to many, but they soon released that it was also elusive. Eventually those at the 'bottom' learned quickly that when their people got to the 'top' they inexplicably preferred to keep the numbers up there low. But that never stopped the people who by now had internalised the lie that they were lacking in their previous state from chasing the dream of immense wealth and status. Even the wealthy harbored a tinge of inadequacy. Invaders may have been asked to leave but their toxins remained present in the souls of our people, including those that made conscious efforts to unlearn the lies they had been trained to believe found that it was a daily struggle of unlearning destructive behaviours.

She was not at a point in her life where she could bribe judges or magistrates, to ensure her recruitment went smooth sailing, and realistically if she had the type of influence to bride a judge, a job as a secretary would not have been the career she would have pursued. Makesa resolved to investigate who the right people were for her to be to contact, and she would get this information from workers starting from the bottom up in organisations. Makesa was committed to searching till she found a person in every office, who could apply any necessary pressure for her to get a job or at least be an advocate for her, when the time came to consider her application for a job. She knew she would not be the only one taking this initiative. She suspected a good number of students would have direct contacts anyway, that meant less options for her, which was why it was imperative that she begin planning her path as early as possible. She started with the courts, Makesa was always interested in the law, had Shikulu not assigned her nursing she would have chosen working within the field of law in any form. She started her enquiries with cleaners of the buildings, she would arrive at the court houses, and engage the cleaners, and all the people no one saw, with a bottle of cold coca cola in hand and a bread roll. Greetings and asking after their families first Makesa would find a way to weave in questions regarding who had the power to employ secretaries. She would also enquire if there were any whispers of secretaries that might be leaving. After her warmup routine she found most were more than happy to share information with her about specific people who would be receptive to listening to her request and who she needed watch out for because they would only be wasting her time.

After a month when the post was delivered, among all the letters was a large A4 brown envelope that stood out from all the others. Looking at the manila envelope it was obvious the letter was sent from abroad, the number of stamps used as well as the typing were some indicators of that. Makesa knew her results had finally arrived, she did not wait for others to come home to offer moral support before opening the letter, by now hard experiences had numbed her so if she was nervous in that moment her body did not know it. When she opened the letter, the heading written in clear dark font was 'Pitman', they had been told it was a distinguished institution whose results were recognised worldwide, a certificate with their name on it was worth its weight in gold as a result. She quickly scanned the paper and saw the result written clearly 'First-class award in shorthand'. She was ecstatic and rang Mwazi at work, which was not like them at all, they had a rule to always respect each other's workplaces and this rule was not unique to them. For most working people, family phone calls at work or even an informal visit of a family member at work were not considered good practice. She shared the good news with him, and he was happy, but could not speak further. Which she did not mind just as long as one of the most important people in her life knew her news first. She thought to call him first also, because of his unwavering support of her in general.

She immediately embarked upon job hunting and found it a challenge, she learned quickly that the field was much smaller than she had anticipated. But she felt confident that if she kept looking for an opening even one slightly beneath her experience and qualifications, she could turn that opportunity into an avenue to work her way up. Her constant checking and persistence paid off in the form of nepotism. One of Shikulu's students recognised her at the courthouse. He was a Lawyer, and this recognition proved to be a significant shift in her fortune because as soon as he discovered in conversation that, she was looking for employment he offered to check for her while at work. He took her number and promised to call if he heard anything as among the court clerks and stenographers as he went about his day. He assured her that there was high demand for those roles and suggested it could be an opportunity to get her foot in the door.

The next morning Makesa's contact rang and asked her to come to the courthouse immediately, as they needed cover for one of their regular stenographers. It was sudden but with a house full of family, childcare was not her first worry. He explained quickly as he was busy, that the woman in charge of the rota had been talking about needing a person urgently and word got back to him through the other staff he had asked to keep their ear to the ground for any jobs going in the office. He explained that he knew the woman in charge of recruitment and passed on her details to her assuring the manager that Makesa was an extremely talented person and could do the job easily. His position was the only reason the manager entertained his suggestion; it was also her insurance in case the person ended up being a complete disaster. Makesa decided not to share with him that she had no idea what taking court notes practically involved, he knew her shorthand was the fastest in her college, because she had told him that, but she had no practical experience. Makesa came up with a plan to write everything very fast and fix any layout issues after the fact. There was no sense in alarming her friend at this stage as there was nothing to indicate her concerns were without a solution she could find.

Chibe chibe umwenso nimfwa – What will be will be, living in fear is as good as death.

She put on her smartest dress, left the children with her family at home, and drove to the local courthouse. When she arrived, she was directed to where she needed to be, as she walked into the office, Makesa was immediately aware of the busy atmosphere that dominated in the office, every part appeared to be moving. She decided to look like she belonged so that if anyone needed her to step into any situation, they would feel confident that she could. As soon as the manager known informally as Ba Na Mutinta clocked her, she walked up to Makesa straight away. This was her realm and though it was busy she was in complete control, so much so that a stranger in her space was spotted by her and skashe intended to find out what the stranger's purpose for being in the court office was. It was the local court, and as manager she felt proud of the part she played in this distinguished environment. In that moment, there was the pressing matter of a person in their offices that did not belong. She walked up to the sister who looked altogether too sure of herself and much too eager.

Na (Mother of) Mutinta walked up to Makesa, smiled and asked her what her business was in the court office. Makesa smiled ensuring it looked timid not domineering, she knew she was in the presence of someone who held power and it was not her intention for her introduction to be perceived as antagonising, confrontational or even worse challenging. She responded to the question by explaining that she was there to transcribe in the court, however she had not been given the details of where she needed to be and hoped the good Madam could direct her to the right place. Ba Na Mutinta smiled, after all who did not enjoy reverence. This young lady had started the right way, if she kept this up, she might even get called back for more work. God knows the courts had been sent many useless girls more concerned with wearing lipstick and making themselves visible for a potential husband, when they should have been concerning themselves with doing their work properly. This one wanted to impress a woman, maybe she could do the work.

Trusting her instincts, she also decided she would give the new one a bit more information about the proceedings, however if she was inept, Ba Na Mutinta would have not hesitate in sending her away and dealing with the person who referred her to the distinguished court. Makesa had in hand her spiral shorthand notepad and pens, this impressed her potential recruiter. Na Mutinta directed her to the place she would sit, gave her the tenets of court conduct for someone in her position and left her in the room awaiting the arrival of lawyers, defendants, judges and others that would be in attendance.

Makesa loved the smell and prestige of a court room, she took in all its atmosphere and the order the court room commanded despite it being empty. She did not feel invisible or intimidated, she felt acutely aware of the importance of each role played by everyone in the court. The notes she would take were vital, the judge, lawyers, defendants, witnesses, everyone in that room had purpose and it was important. She was in her element in that room. As long as everyone who entered that space did their job well, the integrity of the process would be preserved. Makesa loved that idea; she was the product of order and discipline. But this was also her blind spot it would take her many years to appreciate that the new system whilst unlike their justice system, for all its procedures and imagery of fairness and justice, was in fact not always a just system. In reality it failed to accomplish its goal to remain true to its written codes of integrity and impartiality, it was at best orderly unfairness, aesthetically pleasing injustice. The beauty of the courts, the foreign majesty, the authority in that moment and for many years to come was intoxicating for her. This was where she belonged, this was where she would grow and for the first time in her life, all her planning and ambition tipped over into a ruthless desire to remain in that space, whatever the cost.

At the end of her workday, Makesa sought out Ba Na Mutinta, she knew that would be the best place to start her charm offensive. Na Mutinta saw her coming a mile away. She knew ambition when she saw it and realised this might also be a very good opportunity to fix another problem she had. Her current team was better than the one she had inherited. However, there was one problem. Among her team was a lady who was from another land, this lady had been inherited from the previous regime and she enjoyed the benefits that came with undermining Black people. She was not the first to take advantage of a racist system, and that was not the problem Na Mutinta had with her. The problem was that this woman was incapable of doing the job, the issue was not incompetence rather, it was simply that she had no idea how to carry out any of the administrative tasks required of a person in her position. Every morning the woman came into work and chatted, she could not type, and had no experience working in an office. She appeared to understand her limitations because she decided that her role was instead to make delicious food for the staff to eat and the manager found this unacceptable. The courts were not a place for people to decide what their function would be, it was an orderly structure. Na Mutinta was forced to frequently call-in extra help when her usual ladies were swamped with their daily workload and therefore unable to carry the office lay about. To the manager what was worse was the fact that snack lady had never made any attempt to learn the job for as long as she had worked in the court offices. A job working in the courthouse was an honour and this woman treated it as though it were a flight of fancy, a convenient distraction or a delightful project to discuss in her social settings. While this arrangement worked very well for snack lady, it was not working for the entire office.

The invaders had left after a long struggle and disorder would not be the result of our people taking over. If chaos overrun the courthouse, it would not be on Na Mutinta's watch or in her name. That is why she decided that ruthless ambition would be what would set them all free. First, she had to make sure she was right about Makesa. This involved pretending Makesa had managed to charm her into getting regular work, in lieu of a permanent contract. The manager promised Makesa that she was top of the list for future permanent work consideration. This promise also ensured that Makesa's work would remain of a high standard while she worked there. For the manager whatever way this went she was winning. First thing Monday morning Na Mutinta called her new staff member to her office, her plan was to keep her working close to the judges, she wanted them to become addicted to the efficiency she knew would follow Makesa's daily work.

Makesa did not disappoint, she appeared unfriendly but only because she was the type of person that preferred to work, rather than worry about ingratiating herself with her colleagues. Her attitude meant that the other ladies failed to warm to her. For the manager that was a good thing, her staff had all been duped into receiving treats in return for stretching their workload to include snack lady's work, even the suggestion of moving the woman along made the other women in the office jump to her defense. Which is why she was pleased Makesa did not crave to be part of the office circle. Na Mutinta knew that Makesa's self-exclusion from the whole, would make ousting the thorn in her side that much easier. Judges soon noticed the change in the standard and quality of work produced, everything including the speed with which it was completed was better and they were full of praise. To Makesa's annoyance snack lady, would always find a way of worming into those conversations giving the appearance of having had something to do with the changes. She also indirectly implied she had spear headed the new direction. That infuriated Makesa and Na Mutinta who could only watch as they burned with rage. This carried on for two months, and Na Mutinta allowed it before finally pulling Makesa aside. She shared in a very cavalier way that two of the office secretaries would be taking some time off. Hoping that Makesa would understand where she was going with this she carried on, explaining that during that period she needed Makesa to focus only on her work and only what she had be directed to do by the manager. She added that when it came time for the other secretaries to go on holiday, she would put together a weekly Rota for all the staff to ensure all aspects of the two women's responsibilities were covered while they were away. She reiterated that Makesa refuse to deviate from the tasks she would be assigned during that period.

Before long the first week of the other secretaries' holiday was upon them. Snack lady arrived with goodies as usual, and just as she had done before Makesa politely declined and continued transcribing. A young man from the court room entered the office, he appeared to have been running, looking very stressed he asked where the stenographer was. There were two people in the room at the time and Makesa knew she was not due in court. A quick scan of the Rota showed that the office lady of leisure was due in court. She was mortified, she had never done it before and immediately turned to Makesa and instructed her to go instead. Makesa declined and explained that the notes she was transcribing also came with a pressing deadline. Snack lady burst into tears, this was not new, and it was at that point that Makesa realised permanent employment was impending. Makesa suggested as she carried on typing that snack lady pick up a note pad and head into the court room as causing delays with proceedings was frowned upon.

Snack lady looked at Makesa and the realisation that she would not help her hit hard. She was angry, outraged and for the first time remembered that she was perceived higher the African woman before her. Her inner entitlement and superiority found its way to the surface as she waited momentarily for Makesa to come to her senses. Snack lady planned to tell the other women when they returned, this young lady would learn her lesson by losing a job she had only started a few months ago. Snack lady thought this to herself as she walked toward the court room. When she entered the room, the magnitude of what occurred in that space overwhelmed her, some of the orderlies that worked in court directed her to her assigned seat, but all the hints or goodwill in the world would not be able to help her takes notes in court on that day. Snack lady had worked there long enough to understand the importance of the role she was now expected to cover and the consequences of the disruption her inability to perform her function would cause everyone. Thinking about the people whose lives she might destroy became too much and she in that moment snack lady descended into a meltdown just as soon as everyone had begun to walk in. The Judge having compassion and also not understanding what was going on asked that someone else replace her immediately. The orderly was asked to get a replacement as soon as possible while they waited. He ran to the office and told Makesa that she was required to go into court room, Makesa knew that refusing would have been career suicide. Instead, she made the decision to quickly brief snack lady on the mountain of work she had to transcribe that day, the numerous tapes, on a number of cases, including who the work needed to be handed into when complete. Makesa then ran to the court room where she would spend the entire day. Snack lady's bad day was nowhere near over, in fact it was about to get worse. Makesa was a very fast typist and having deliberately been given a lot of work to get through by her manager, snack lady was not going to rest for a moment that day, she knew the target given her was unobtainable for someone with her lack of skill. In desperation snack lady rang the other women on holiday because she was sure they would come in to help her. But work rules and security at the court, were such that people were not free to come and go they pleased, she was on her own.

Snack lady was loved by the other two women, her regular treats had managed to conjure fierce loyalty for her in her work colleagues. Even the office orderlies thought Makesa was cruel, and though she was not oblivious to the hostility, she simply did not care. The plan that she lived by had nothing to do with any of them. She was aware of their cowardice in failing to accept that maybe management no longer wanted the lady of leisure, and the fact they found it easier to blame her only made her respect for them diminish further. Manager conveniently made her presence scarce that day, behaviour that was unusual for her and was not missed by the staff, everyone wondered if the current unkind treatment of snack lady had been contrived by the manager and Makesa, some even whispered as much. Yet as much as they liked snack lady no one was prepared to risk their jobs by vocalising their suspicions about their manager. For that day, snack lady could either rise to the challenge after working in that office for five years or accept the following days would be a living nightmare for her.

At the end of that workday Makesa left on time and at the corner of her eye, she saw snack lady typing with what sounded like her two index fingers. For her part there was no reveling in her colleague's misery, but she would have been lying if she said she felt even remotely sorry for her. The absurdity of going to work, to avoid doing work was a concept she was not familiar with. The following morning when Makesa arrived for work, she was told that snack lady had phoned in sick, and she was on her own for the time being in the office. The judges whose work had been delayed were apoplectic, they insisted Makesa kindly redo the work as it had been badly done and was full of errors, then there were the costly delays. Manager stepped in and explained to the judges that Makesa was an amazing find for the court but there was no budget for her, she then added that the court office had staff who were paid but not productive as judges were now finding out. The judges paused, it turned out snack lady was the wife of an important man. The senior of the two decided that the work they did was far more important than pleasing a friend, they asked manager to employ Makesa straight away as her good work had not gone unnoticed. They assured manager that they would find a solution for their snack lady problem. But for now, they needed the backlog addressed as a matter of urgency

They need not have concerned themselves, the humiliation snack lady felt having been humbled around people she had been groomed to believe, she was better than was more than enough. What had transpired that day meant that she would not return to the courts to pretend to work ever again. She never explained the full extent of her awful day to her husband, nor did she tell their house cleaners who she sometimes confided in. Snack lady had come to rely on them as a result of the loneliness she felt in her early months when they first arrived in the country. As for her friends and country people, discussing her humiliation to them was out of the question. When she arrived home on that difficult day, she explained to her husband that she was tired of working and keeping the office environment pleasant for her colleagues every day. She had come to accept that the native people were indeed too much work, possibly unteachable and the exhaustion she felt that day was proof of that. Her husband not considered an expat but ranked more senior than the Indigenous people, knew exactly what his wife's abilities were. But her boredom and homesickness had become his problem, loving his wife, and wanting her to be happy, he made arrangements to keep her busy while he was at work. In truth this was not the married life she had envisaged. But her husband had been given an opportunity to work abroad, and goodness knows when they were still in their homeland, they had both bragged endlessly about the new position and the prestige of being called upon by invaders to manage positions they deemed beneath them and required another group of people to assist instead.

In her heart she felt the idea other humans were better than was ridiculous and if it was up to her, she would have told the truth about what the invaders really were, but there was little incentive for her to rock the boat. Besides her actions reflected on her husband and she had no interest or intention of harboring an unemployed man as husband. This was not their fight, and she did not care to make it their concern. In the morning they discussed plans for her next venture, they both knew she preferred not to work among their people. There were enough dramatics when they all gathered socially. All the other wives went on and on about being professional women and snack lady's background was not professional. They never said it directly, but occasionally they talked down to her and on more than one occasion took to over explaining things in conversation for her benefit. She could not stand any of them, but they were her people, and she was abroad far from family. She felt compelled to play along. Snack lady was not a fighter or a disrupter, she did not have a clue how to handle herself among snobs. Working in the courts had been her cover, it had bought her some respectability among them, not much but enough to stop them obnoxiously explaining things she had not asked to be explained with those irritating smiles on their faces. She really could not stand them. Now she needed to find another cover to use as an achievement talking point in her social circles.

Meanwhile Makesa was finally in, there was no doubt in her mind that she could do the job very well. Her had found a job that not only made her feel like it was where she belonged but also came with fantastic employment benefits and protections was a wonderful feeling. Makesa had no plans of putting her employment benefits to good use, but it was good to know that if she wanted to, she could. That evening Mwazi and Makesa sat down to update their financial plan to include how they would support their family members in need of education. They were committed to Shikulu's vision, their plan was lacking the detail he had laid out, and they were having to improvise and work with what they had. They both agreed that every year because their house so full of people that they would take their children away for a week, it was not much time alone as a family, but it was what they had decided they could afford. They sent word home letting family know that when they were ready, they would call for the next person to come and live with them. Everything was finally beginning to fall in place for them.

Printed in Great Britain
by Amazon